Noble Metals (Metals #1)

L.A. WITT

Copyright Information

NOBLE METALS

L.A. WITT

Chapter 1

The dark-haired stranger stepped into the saloon, and every whore's head turned, including mine.

Strangers were nothing new in Seattle, not since the stampede had begun a year or so ago, but anyone walking through that door was a potential john. After several slow nights in a row, none of us wasted time sizing up new arrivals.

As I searched him for tells—something to hint if he was here for a drink, a game of cards, or a companion for the night—I had to admit I was intrigued. Gladys had said that if you'd seen one stampeder, you'd seen them all, but once in a while, someone stood out from the crowd.

Like this one.

From behind the bar where I was wiping down glasses, I watched him. He looked tired and cold just like everyone else, but he carried himself like he was already on his way back from the Yukon with a pocket full of gold. Even as he brushed the rainwater off the sleeves of his heavy overcoat and held his hat outside the door to shake it out, he had a dignified air that didn't often find its way into Ernest's saloon and brothel.

Apparently satisfied his coat and hat were dry enough, he came all the way in, carrying a large pack on his shoulders and a locked wooden box in his hand.

He *strolled* toward the bar. I couldn't decide if he didn't have a care in the world or if he was damned certain the rest of the world would be wise to get out of his way. On his way across the warm, if stuffy, saloon, he didn't even seem to notice Frances's and Anna's coquettish smiles.

Aside from a day's worth of shadow on his jaw, he was clean-shaven, and his dark hair was only slightly tousled from his hat, which he set on the bar. He shrugged off his pack, then his coat, revealing a finely embroidered waistcoat that had clearly been tailored to fit his narrow waist. Well dressed. Not rich, but certainly not destitute. Still too early to say if he'd come here for a whore, but from the looks of him, he could afford one, and he was showing no interest in the girls, so I casually inched closer to where he was sitting.

Ernest leaned on the bar. "What'll it be?"

The stranger peeled off his leather gloves and laid them beside his hat. "Your best cognac, please."

Oh, dear Lord, he had a voice like the cognac he wanted.

Ernest laughed. "What city d'you think you're in, son?" He gestured at the rows of uniform bottles on the wall. "Whiskey or brandy are the best you're going to find here."

The newcomer scowled, then made a dismissive yet so *elegant* gesture. "Whiskey will do fine. A double, please."

Ernest beckoned to me. "Robert, get over here and pour the man a drink."

"Yes, sir." I joined him, and the newcomer met my eyes but only for a second.

Clearing his throat, he shifted his attention to Ernest while I poured his drink. "Do you know where a man might look if he wants to round up a team to head north?"

"Heading north?" Ernest sniffed. "You and every man in this town. Ain't you heard the ground up there's running out of gold? The last two months, every stampeder who's come back through here's been empty-handed."

My stomach sank at the reminder of the dwindling gold fields. Some said the gold would all be picked clean by spring, and those who left now to struggle over that hellish pass into the Yukon would be weeping into frozen, barren soil for their trouble. With winter just around the bend, those of us still itching to make the journey were losing hope by the day.

"I've heard the rumors." The stranger offered a tight-lipped smile. "But I'm not concerned about that."

Ernest eyed him, then shrugged. "Well, you'll find the men you're looking for hanging around the docks down by the outfitters. But watch your pockets—there's as many thieves down there as men who could help you."

"But there *are* men looking to go north?"

"Aye. Dozens of 'em who'll join any party led by a man who'll pay them." Ernest turned to me. "How about that drink?"

I slid the double whiskey across the bar. The stranger briefly met my eyes again, and his taut expression warmed to something a little friendlier.

He turned back to Ernest. "I'm also in need of a room. I expect to be gone tomorrow, so—"

"You'll have to speak to Beatrice." Ernest gestured across the barroom to where his wife, the brothel's madam, peered at everyone over her teacup. "She's in charge of the whores and the rooms."

The stranger glanced over his shoulder. "I don't suppose there are beds available with*out* company?"

Ernest shook his head. "Not in this hotel."

"Very well." The stranger nodded and raised his glass. "I'll finish my drink and be on my way, then."

Ernest left him to his drink. I should have done the same, but I may as well have been knee-deep in mud.

The stranger studied me as I studied him. He didn't have the same hunger in his eyes as the other stampeders. Oh, there was something in his eyes, something I couldn't quite put my finger on, but he lacked the palpable gold fever so many men in this town had these days.

I cleared my throat. "You're setting out in the morning?"

"Well, once I find a man or two who can accompany me, and of course some equipment to haul my gear." Clicking his tongue, he shook his head. "Ridiculous, this requiring a damned year's worth of provisions for each man just to get into Canada. Any man worth his salt could easily survive on half that."

"I've heard it isn't true."

His eyebrows rose. "Is that so?"

I nodded. "They say it's just the outfitters' way of making money." I gestured in the general direction of the docks. "Trouble is, the boats are in on it too, and they won't let anyone on board without it. Only the airships will."

He snorted. Into his glass, he muttered, "And what man who hasn't already struck it rich can *afford* an airship ticket?"

I laughed quietly. As he swallowed the whiskey with a grimace, I glanced around, then leaned on the bar and lowered my voice. "So you're traveling alone at the moment?"

"Aren't most men who walk into a brothel?"

"I…well, no. Some have just broken away from their—" I waved a hand. "Listen, the men down at the docks, whatever you'll pay them to come with you, I'll do it for half."

He blinked. "I beg your pardon?"

I couldn't quite believe I'd blurted it out that way, but I didn't take it back. He was a stranger, but he had two things I needed enough to take a risk that would've been deemed foolish by most men: the means to get to Dawson City and a vacancy for a team member.

"Half," I said in spite of my dry mouth. "I'll help you haul your gear, dig, everything, for half of what you'd pay them."

He stared at me for a moment and then chuckled. "Might be a bit cold and grueling for someone of your profession, don't you think?"

I glared at him. "I'm only a whore because it keeps me fed. I came to Seattle for the same reason you did."

The stranger shook his head and then brought his glass up to his lips again. "Oh, I doubt that very much."

"Why?" I growled. "Don't think I want to find gold just like the next man?"

"No, no, not that." He gave another quiet chuckle. "But I assure you, we're not going up there for the same reasons." He set his glass on the bar again. "Why aren't you on your way to Dawson City already?"

My cheeks burned. "Because my brothers and I lost the money for our provisions. Didn't even have enough to get back to Montana."

"And you think you'll make that money in Dawson City?" He eyed me. "Plenty of men come back poorer than they left, you know."

"I know. Been stuck working here for six months now, so I've got enough money saved to hold me over. What I want is to go to Dawson City, but I can't handle that much gear myself, and I can't afford to buy a mech, never mind pay someone to operate it."

He pursed his lips but said nothing.

"I'd have gone with any other team, but men look at me"—I gestured at myself—"and don't think I'm strong enough for the journey. I'm small, but I am *not* weak."

He rolled a sip of whiskey around in his mouth as he looked me over. As much as he could see above the bar, anyway.

I pushed my shoulders back. "Listen, I can pull my weight. And I'm desperate. I can't go back to Montana. The stampede will only last so much longer, and then this place will be back to the logging town it was before. And I've seen what happens to loggers. I'll risk freezing off my fingers and toes to get to Dawson City for a fool's chance at riches before you'll find me working in a logging camp."

He glanced around the brothel, his gaze pausing on three of the girls trying to charm men into their beds, then raised an eyebrow at me. "This is preferable to logging?" Before I could reply, he nodded. "I suppose it is, isn't it?"

"It is. And I won't be able to make a living in here once this stampede ends." I cursed the desperation in my voice and in my situation. "That could be in a month, six months, a year. Who knows? But if I have any chance of finding gold, I can't wait much longer."

"You may already be too late. The barkeep said himself the gold fields are dwindling."

"That isn't stopping you."

"I'm not interested in gold."

Then why...

But I shrugged. "I'll take my chances. I didn't come here, lose my shirt, and whore myself for six months just to turn around and go home."

The stranger's brow furrowed. "And you said you came here from Montana?"

I nodded.

"How many years in Montana?"

"Twenty. Lived there my whole life before I came here."

"So you know what harsh winters are like," he said, more to himself than to me.

"Probably better than most of the men you'll find down on the pier."

He swirled his drink slowly, watching the liquid slosh inside the glass. "What did you do for work before you came here?"

"My father is a tanner. I worked for him and on my grandfather's farm."

The stranger looked me up and down again, running his thumb across his lower lip. This was when most men would inform me they didn't think I was quite strong enough, quite solid enough to handle the journey, never mind the mining at the end of it. That, or they'd leer at me and say of *course* I could join them, at which point I'd realize I'd be out in the middle of nowhere with these men rather than in the relative safety of the brothel, and I'd think better of my offer.

The stranger opened his mouth to speak, but just as he did, heavy boots tromped across the planks outside the door. Out of habit, I turned my head. He did as well, and when three men appeared—as well dressed as he was—he turned back toward the bar, swearing under his breath.

The other three talked amongst themselves, their voices low and their eyes darting around the room.

The stranger glanced at the floor beside him, and something scraped quietly. Wood on wood, as if he'd nudged the locked box with his foot.

One of the new arrivals stared right at the stranger, and then turned to the others. They exchanged muffled words until one gestured for the others to follow him.

As they left the way they'd come, the stranger glanced over his shoulder again. He exhaled hard and reached for his glass again.

A knot tightened in my stomach. "You know them?"

He studied me as he took another sip of whiskey. "We're...colleagues of sorts."

Colleagues? Of sorts? What did that—

"I think I'll stay here after all." He glanced back at the empty doorway, and then his glass clinked on the polished bar. "How much do you charge for a night?"

I gulped. "Um, for the bed? Or the company?"

He held my gaze. "Either or."

"Five…five dollars for the bed." I almost choked on the words. "An extra three if I'm not in it."

His expression turned to one of amusement, his broad smile crinkling the corners of his eyes. "It's more expensive to sleep alone, is it?"

I gave a casual shrug in spite of my pounding heart. "If you sleep alone, I have to go find a place for myself."

"Point taken." His gaze darted toward the door. Then he drained his drink and slid the glass back across the bar. "In that case…" He reached into the pocket of his trousers and withdrew a few bills and coins. He counted some out, then put it beside the glass. "Fifteen cents for the drink, eight dollars for the bed. Unaccompanied, if you please."

My heart sank, and I tried not to show my disappointment or take it as an insult that he'd declined my services. After all, men who were interested in me were few and far between compared to those who came for the girls—that was why I also tended bar.

I collected the money and nodded toward Beatrice. "I'll let her know you'll be staying with us tonight."

He smiled. "Thank you."

Once Beatrice had taken her cut and given me what was left, I offered to carry his pack and box, but he declined, hoisting the former onto his shoulder and clutching the latter's handle.

I led him out of the bar area to the creaking staircase. Upstairs, amorous sounds came from Catherine's room, and I was sure I heard Gladys's voice in there too. Good. If they were working together tonight, as they often did, maybe I could talk Beatrice into letting me occupy Gladys's room for a few hours.

I was being paid without having to work for it, but I didn't want to let this man out of my sight while I was still holding on to the hope that he might take me up on my offer to join his team. On the other hand, the three men who'd made him nervous made me a little nervous too. What was I getting myself into?

As I led him down the hall, dusty amber bulbs dimmed and brightened along the crown molding like they were connected to my pounding heart instead of the wires that drew our electricity from the city's hydroelectric plant. When finely dressed men casually pursued other finely dressed men into barrooms, there was reason to be concerned. Perhaps he was a criminal. More than a few thieves and crooks had swindled their way through Seattle to Alaska and up the deadly Chilkoot Trail, sneaking across the border into the Yukon to escape or to wreak havoc on the miners in Dawson City. The red-coated North-West Mounted Police *didn't* always get their man.

My hands shook as I drew my room key out of my pocket. I unlocked open the door and gestured for him to go ahead. Then I walked past him and lit the kerosene lamp. "There's an electric light in here. I'm not fond of it, since it blinks and dims all the time, but you're welcome to it."

"The kerosene is fine," he said in that cognac-smooth voice.

I pulled open a bureau drawer to find the few things I'd take with me to wherever I'd be sleeping tonight. "I'll leave the key here on the bureau. Beatrice asks that you're out by quarter past nine in the morning, and—"

The door clicked shut. I turned around.

From across the tiny room, in the faintly flickering light, our eyes met.

The stranger grinned. "Am I safe in assuming that paying your surcharge doesn't *preclude* a night's company?"

Chapter 2

"I...what?" I shook my head. "I mean, why would you pay extra for—"

"Merely keeping up appearances, my lad." He set the wooden box on the floor and toed it up against the wall, then eased his pack off his shoulders and draped his jacket over it. My mind and heart were both racing, but our eyes met, and something in me stilled. There was nothing threatening or menacing in his slight smile, and when he took a step toward me, I didn't draw back.

"The walls in every city have ears," he said, "and there are loose lips between this town and the Yukon that can be heard all the way to Chicago. Three dollars is a small price to pay for a little discretion, don't you think?" The three faces downstairs flashed through my mind again, but vanished when his long fingers went to the first button on his waistcoat. "I assure you, I have every intention of using the services I paid extra not to use." One eyebrow rose, as did the corner of his mouth. "Assuming that's all right with you?"

I cleared my throat. "Um, of course. Certainly." I started unbuttoning my shirt, but paused. "What about going with you? To Dawson City?"

The man eyed me, and his fingers stopped on a button. An odd smile—midway between puzzled and amused—pulled at his slim lips, and he lowered his hands, tugging at his waistcoat as if he'd meant to straighten it, not remove it. "You're already being paid extra, but you still want to bargain?"

"I don't think you realize how badly I want out of this town."

Folding his arms loosely across his partially unbuttoned waistcoat, he tilted his head. "You'll go for half the wages the men on the pier would require?"

"Yes. And split the cost of a mech."

He pursed his lips. "You can afford a ticket to Ketchikan?"

I nodded. "Yes."

"Your own provisions?"

"And then some."

It took all I had not to squirm under the weight of his stare—his long, scrutinizing pauses were unnerving.

"You can afford a ticket and provisions," he said after a moment, "but you can't go back to Montana?"

I gritted my teeth. "I didn't say it was money keeping me from going home."

"I see." Then he gave a sharp nod. "Very well. I'll hire you."

Excitement and relief swelled beneath my breastbone. "Thank you."

"We'll acquire our provisions tomorrow morning and leave on the next boat to Ketchikan." He smiled thinly and resumed unbuttoning his waistcoat. "Now, about tonight's arrangement…"

I was so thrilled about my good fortune, I couldn't even figure out what to do next until, in a smooth, mesmerizing motion, he pushed the first button through its keeper. As he unfastened the next one, I realized I needed to do the same and reached for the next button of my shirt.

My work was, in its best moments, passionless, my body going through the motions like the provision-laden spidery brass mechs that marched through the streets outside on their way to Dawson City. But I'd wanted him from the start, and the fact that he'd just made himself my ticket to the Yukon made me want him even more. Made me want to *enjoy* him.

Piece by piece, he removed his silk and wool, and with each finely tailored layer, he stripped away my ability to think. He was the most beautiful thing that had come through Seattle in the last year, with shoulders cut from marble and a smooth chest and stomach above narrow hips. Sparse, dark hair fanned out from the middle of his chest, simply begging my fingers to run through it, and a thin strip below his navel guided my eyes below his belt a moment before his hands began unfastening his trousers.

My own hands were clumsy. *What is* wrong *with you, Robert?* No john had ever had this effect on me, rendering me so useless that I had only managed to remove my shirt and boots by the time he was completely, gloriously naked. But then, he was my long-sought-after escape from this place—I supposed that warranted some unusual infatuation.

Stroking himself slowly, he whispered, "Get on your knees."

An all-too-familiar dread constricted my throat. Few things made me want to gag more than sucking unwashed men who spent all their money on brothels and not a penny on baths.

I swallowed hard and knelt in front of him. He'd paid for this. I wouldn't deny him. His hand left his cock and rested in my hair as I dutifully took him between my lips. To my surprise, he smelled lightly of soap—he'd been to Smith's for a bath, I could tell by the scent—and a spine-tingling masculine muskiness. His skin was vaguely salty, and he was almost too thick for my jaw to accommodate. I shivered and took him as deep as I could.

I'd never experienced such a thing myself—I always gave, never received—but men rarely complained, and his groans of approval made my own trousers almost too tight to bear.

Never before had I craved someone like this. I'd only known a man's touch when there was money exchanged, but this time, the money didn't matter. I wanted him to be satisfied with what I did because I wanted to please him.

This was unprecedented. But I couldn't question it. I was too occupied with giving him the sum total of everything I knew, every way I'd learned to make a man—

"Wait, stop," he whispered hoarsely. When I looked up, he nodded toward my bed. "Turn around."

I jumped to my feet and unfastened my trousers. The man obviously wasn't new to this, because he knew exactly what purpose the white bottle beside my bed served. He reached for it and poured some of the slippery, clear liquid into his palm as I stripped off the rest of my clothes.

Per his command, I got on my knees on the bed, and my nameless john knelt behind me. He pressed a cool, slicked finger against my entrance, and I closed my eyes as it slipped into me. These days, I didn't require much help to relax enough for a man to fuck me, but he took his time anyway, easing me open with one finger, two, a third. Even after I'd relaxed, he didn't stop. Much as I wanted to beg for his cock, I bit my tongue. He'd paid for his pleasure, not mine. And besides, his fingers—slippery and gentle— created a degree of pleasure I'd never experienced before. My breath kept catching in my throat as his fingers eased in and out. Sometimes he'd part them to stretch my entrance, other times they simply moved. In and out, in and out, until I was a breath away from begging him to fuck me.

He withdrew his fingers completely, and I moaned in both protest and anticipation. As he reached for the white bottle again, I shivered, sucking in a sharp hiss of breath through gritted teeth.

The bottle clinked on the bedside table, and the mattress shifted behind me.

I closed my eyes as he pressed himself against me. Even after he'd fingered me until I thought I'd lose my mind, he was in no hurry to force himself inside me. He slid the head of his cock into me, then pulled out, and I whimpered softly at the absence of him. A second later, he pressed in again, and this time he pushed deeper, and I leaned back to take even more of him. To take all of him. I was used to some painful friction while my body accepted a hurried man, and more often than not, by the time I started to enjoy it, he'd be done. Not this time, though. I had never taken a man's cock after being so deliciously prepared for it, and every stroke was pure ecstasy.

I couldn't stop myself from rocking in time with his thrusts, silently begging him for more. Some patrons didn't like that, refusing to relinquish even the most minuscule amount of control, but he simply moaned and thrust harder.

Then he shifted, leaning over me and resting his hands on the mattress beside mine. He kissed the side of my neck, and I pulled in a ragged breath, which I promptly lost when he thrust deep and hard into me.

His chin was coarse against the back of my shoulder, unlike the soft warmth of his lips and breath. "Tell me your name."

Surely he'd heard it downstairs, but what he asked for, he received. I found enough air to whisper, "Robert."

"Robert," he growled, and my name had never sounded so filthy. "Mmm, I love what you're doing, Robert."

21

I shivered and tried to remember what I was doing. Fortunately, my body kept moving of its own accord, meeting him thrust for thrust until tears stung my eyes.

"Do you like that, Robert?"

Moaning, I let my head fall forward, so lost in desire, I couldn't focus on anything except enjoying what he did, on the way he slid so easily in and out of me, and breathed on me, and promised with every stroke a climax to end all climaxes.

I wavered between holding back and letting go, falling apart a little more every time his cock met that eye-watering spot.

Shifting my weight onto one trembling arm, I reached down and closed my fingers around my painfully hard cock. I gasped, tensed, and a second later, he too gasped. With a low, guttural growl, he thrust even harder. Hot tears ran down my cheeks as he drove me to that promised climax, and my eyes rolled back as I spent into my palm.

Just as my vision began to clear and his strokes became uncomfortably intense, he groaned, forced himself all the way inside me, and shuddered. He was buried to the hilt, not an inch of my backside absent the heat of his flesh, and every twitch and tremor resonated through me.

Panting, he kissed the side of my neck. "You're worth easily twice what you charge, Robert."

"I don't know." I licked my lips. "I think I should be paying you." I'd never been so satisfied in my life, and how strange that such satisfaction came from a patron who'd paid for the right to do as he pleased to my body all night. A patron who'd paid extra so no one would know. And no one had to know. I wouldn't say a word to anyone unless it was to him, and those words would be "please, please, do it all again."

And before long, he *did* do it all again.

~*~

The next morning, I watched from my bed as he buckled his belt over his trousers. My body ached from making sure he'd gotten his money's worth last night, though truth be told, I was still certain I should have been paying him.

As I buttoned my shirt, I said, "You never did tell me your name."

He sat on the edge of the bed and leaned down to pull on his boots. "John."

I laughed. "You and every man who comes through this room."

That gave him pause, and he chuckled. "My mother must have known what kind of man I'd be one day." He glanced at me. "Didn't think to use a false name, though. I'll have to remember that next time."

Next time. Jealousy flared in my chest, but I quickly doused it. He was no different than any man who'd paid me for an evening's company. Or rather, he wouldn't be once we'd returned from Dawson City. And I was no more to him than I was to any of them. A whore, a night's entertainment.

"Well, I doubt anyone in this town would think twice. Men bed in the same rooms and tents all the time for lack of vacancy elsewhere."

"They don't generally bed down together in brothels, though," he said dryly.

"Generally, no."

"No matter." He pulled the cuff of his trousers over his laced boot. "But I do appreciate the discretion." Remembering his "colleagues of sorts" who'd come into the bar last night, I gave a quiet sound of acknowledgment.

I leaned down and found my own trousers on the floor. "You said last night you weren't looking for gold. What did you mean? Why else would you go to a gold field?"

He smiled. "I'm searching for platinum."

"In a gold field?"

"Yes." He pulled a brass pocket watch from his breast pocket. "And it's nearly nine, so we shouldn't wait." As he stood, he nodded toward the bed as if to indicate everything we'd done. "And to be clear, you're traveling with me from here on out, but no one is to know about *this*."

I resisted the urge to roll my eyes. "Understood. Of course." I paused. "Do you think you're the first man on that trail who's bedded me for a fee?"

"Absolutely not. But I'd just as soon not have word of last night's arrangement getting back home."

"Wife?"

"Employer." He watched his fingers buttoning his waistcoat. "I don't need them to know what kind of 'immoral conduct' I engage in."

I nodded. That was no surprise. The men who paid me nearly always demanded total secrecy and discretion.

And if it meant a ticket out of this town and up to the gold fields in the Klondike, I would gladly keep any secret John asked me to.

~*~

"You're sure about this?" Beatrice eyed John warily as he waited for me on the other side of the cardroom.

I nodded and hoisted my pack onto my shoulders.

She scowled, eyes shifting toward me. "He don't look like he'd be worth a damn against robbers. Or bears."

"We'll be fine." I glanced at John. "I'd better go. Take care, Beatrice."

"You too, darlin'."

I adjusted my pack, and then followed John out of the saloon and into the rush of men, mechs, and horses. As we made our way through the thick crowd, I stole a few glances at John as Beatrice's voice echoed in my head. Maybe she was right. Faced with a grizzly bear or some determined robbers, John might not be the best ally, but the outfitters down by the piers sold plenty of weapons that would do us just fine. No one went north without a rifle. If we were attacked by something a rifle couldn't stop, no amount of brute strength was going to do us any good anyhow.

And though I wouldn't have admitted it out loud, I was thrilled I wasn't traveling with a giant brute who could best a grizzly. In the past few months, I'd whored myself to plenty of prospectors, but most who were willing to pay for my services weren't men I wanted to work for out on the trail.

John, however, didn't strike me as dangerous, and he had a gentle hand. Maybe he wouldn't break a grizzly's neck, but he probably wouldn't break mine either. A man my size—or in my profession—couldn't be too careful about whom he traveled with.

Down by the waterfront, crowds and congestion gave the appearance of utter chaos, but as we slowly made our way through the outfitters and—once we had our provisions—to the pier, it became clear there was order here. Amidst all the shouting and shuffling, the men working the dock were surprisingly efficient. People moved from outfitter to outfitter, piling provisions on flatbed carts.

Once they had everything, then they acquired a mech, a spidery brass machine that would carry the ton or more of gear over the rugged terrain. When I'd first arrived last year, mechs were issued first, and the result was such disorder, more mechs wound up crashing into each other or buildings before they made it anywhere near the boat to Ketchikan. Since mechs had become the last item a team purchased before boarding the boat, there'd been considerably fewer problems. It was even better after the mech manufacturers had taken over warehouses directly across the street from the pier, so a team needed only to buy their machine, load it, and move it right to the ship instead of trawling through six congested blocks.

I watched an empty mech limp past us. The valves on the front-mounted engine coughed little puffs of steam out the top, and the whole thing rattled as one leg landed badly with every step. I couldn't tell if the leg was bent or if one of its joints was damaged, but something was definitely wrong.

John sneered at it. "*That's* what'll carry our provisions?" He shook his head. "Almost makes you wonder if a horse and sled would make more sense."

"Except the horses don't come with spare parts and repair kits." I gestured at the machine. "So far, I've not heard of anyone having to shoot a mech."

John clapped my shoulder. "Good point. Very good point."

We watched the mech for a moment longer. Two men—one on either side of its front end—guided it, keeping it straight when its damaged leg tried to pull it off course.

John scowled. "Well, let's make sure we bring enough tools and spare parts, shall we?"

I nodded. "Good idea. Do you think you can fix it if it breaks?"

He chuckled, eyes sparkling. "Fix it? Given the time and parts, I could improve it." He nodded sharply at the defective mech. "Better legs. Better efficiency. Maybe even modify the damned thing so it could safely carry itself *and* a couple of passengers."

The idea of riding a mech instead of walking beside it was definitely appealing. "How much time would that take?"

"Sadly, more than I have." He turned to our cart of provisions. "We'll just have to settle for a mech as its manufacturer made it unless I find the opportunity to correct some of its flaws."

"So we will."

We maneuvered our overflowing cart to the mech warehouses. John went in to inspect our mech while I waited outside with our provisions. He left his pack with me but kept the locked box with him. I had to admit, I was curious about its contents. I was curious about a lot of things relating to this stranger, but I supposed I'd learn more eventually. If the stories from other men were to be believed, we'd have plenty of idle time between here and Ketchikan, not to mention Dawson City.

At least it was a pleasant day so far. The sun was shining, glittering on the roads that had been left slick and muddy from yesterday's rain. The air smelled of salt, mud, rain, and horses, not to mention smoke and exhaust from all the boats and ships moving in and out of the harbor. Perhaps the air wasn't perfumed with wine and roses, but it was better than the chemicals of my father's tanning shop. Considering I didn't even have that option anymore, I was happy to take a few hours of breathing the pier-side salt and smoke.

My chest was taut with excitement. Like thousands of other stampeders, my brothers and I had charged into Seattle after someone had sniffed out gold in the Klondike. We'd been among the first to arrive in the swampy logging town sitting in a strip of mud between a lake and Puget Sound, ready to sail and hike north to stake our claims.

Had our provision money not wound up in the pocket of a gambler and the purses of a dozen whores, I'd have been up to the Yukon and back by now with more gold than any man needed.

But at last, I was on my way. The journey would be grueling, and the fields may well have already been stripped bare of gold, but I'd happily dig through the frozen, barren tundra with my bare hands for a fool's chance if it meant no longer whoring myself to men on their way to strike it rich.

I took a deep breath of the stinking air and gazed at the crowd as I waited for John. Amongst the blur of faces and horses, movement caught my eye, and I turned.

My spine crackled with nervous energy. I'd seen that trio before. That nervous energy turned to something colder—they were the three men from the saloon. The "colleagues of sorts" who'd made John nervous.

They stood on the other side of the street, their heads inclined and torsos twisted toward each other in a conspiratorial manner.

"No one is to know about this," John had said within the walls of my room. *"I don't need them to know what kind of 'immoral conduct' I engage in."*

Did that have something to do with these men in particular? I hadn't made the connection then, when my heart had still been pounding with excitement because I was finally en route to the Yukon, but now I wondered. What kind of employer did he mean?

It didn't matter. He had my promise of discretion because he was the one who could get me out of this place. Whatever was between him and those men was none of my business. And it if was dangerous, well, traveling with a stranger who could be involved in something unsavory was no more dangerous than going to the Yukon in the first place.

It was either go or stay here and bed men for money until another came along who was willing to hire me. I'd take my chances.

The door swung open behind me, and John stepped out, the box in one hand and some papers in the other. "All right, everything is secure." He nodded at the cart. "Let's get that inside so they can load the mech. Then we—" He stopped abruptly, and I didn't have to follow his gaze to know what had caught his eye. His leather glove creaked as he tightened his grasp on the box's handle. Cursing under his breath, he gestured sharply inside. "Let's go. Quickly."

I swallowed the questions that raced to the tip of my tongue and instead concentrated on helping him steer the cart into the outfitter's building.

The outfitters loaded the mech, since they knew how to ensure everything was balanced and secure with no wasted space or precarious stacks. While they arranged our provisions, John and I made our way down to the pier. At the edge of the dock, where our boots landed on wood instead of sloshing through mud, I bought my ticket.

While John paid for his, I stared at mine, clutching it in both hands.

This was it.

I had my ticket.

And I was going north.

Chapter 3

John talked like a lonely man. I wondered how long it had been since he'd engaged in comfortable conversation with someone willing to listen. Most people didn't say much to me these days unless it was where to put my mouth or cock, so I was perfectly content to let him talk.

We'd been on the boat for nearly a full day now and had settled into our quarters as the daylight faded. We shared a cramped room with another team, this one comprised of four men. John was loath to leave the tiny quarters for very long, and he refused to go anywhere without that locked box at his side, which only fanned the flame of my curiosity about its contents.

He didn't speak about the box or the men who'd made him nervous this morning. Instead, he regaled me with stories of life in Chicago. Since Seattle was the closest I'd ever been to a real city, I hung on his every word as he told me about factories, riverboats, and buildings as far as the eye could see, with cranes towering over them to erect even more buildings. Automobiles outnumbered horses, and there were machines that made mechs look like useless, primitive toys.

The boat docked for the night near the mouth of Puget Sound, and it was the rumble of the engines and shouts of crewmen that roused me the next morning.

As I stepped down from my bunk, John glanced at me over the top of a book. "Good morning."

"Morning." I leaned against the bulkhead and rubbed my eyes. "Are we moving?"

"Not yet. They're taking on more passengers and cargo, but it sounds like we will be soon."

"Good. Sooner we move, sooner we're off this thing."

He chuckled. "And the sooner we're on the trail with winter coming. These may not be the finest accommodations a man could ask for, but I'd enjoy them while you can."

"Good point." I glanced at the book in his hand. It wasn't the tattered leather-bound journal he'd been writing in last night. "What're you reading? Is that—" I tilted my head and read the embossed gold lettering on the book's spine. "H.G. Wells?"

"It is. You're familiar with him?"

I nodded. "I love him."

John's eyebrows rose, as did one corner of his mouth. "Do you?"

"Yes." I craned my neck, eyeing his pack. "Did you bring any others?"

"Just a handful. The outfitters thought I was a fool for adding extra weight." He shrugged. "But I'd go mad if I didn't have something to read."

"If you want to lighten what's in your pack, I'll carry a few under the condition you let me read them."

"You— Really?"

"Yes, really." I tried not to take offense, but it wasn't easy. "I may be a whore, but I'm not simpleminded. I can read."

"I…oh, I didn't mean to imply…" He shook his head. "My apologies. I simply hadn't thought about it." He dug through his pack and added, "Do you like science fiction?"

"I love it. Someone left *The Time Machine* at the brothel a few months back. I've nearly memorized it."

He glanced at me, grinning like a child. "Have you? I loved that one. Have you read Jules Verne?"

"Some. *Journey to the Center of the Earth* is one of my favorites." I paused. "One of the girls loaned it to me. That and *Twenty Thousand Leagues Under the Sea*."

"Interesting," he murmured, still rummaging through his pack.

"Even whores read, John."

"Well." He withdrew a book and met my eyes. "Perhaps I have a lot to learn about those outside my own profession." Before I could ask what profession that was, he handed me the book. "Since you've read Wells before, you might like this one."

I took it from him. "*The Island of Doctor Moreau*. I've not heard of this one."

"Do tell me how you like it." He smiled. "I haven't read it yet myself."

I returned the smile. "Thank you."

The boat left the dock not long after, and while we gnawed some beef jerky and read, it continued its journey toward the Inside Passage, which would take us to Ketchikan, Alaska.

Holing up in our quarters and reading on our racks was fine for a while, but soon the seas got rough enough to make my stomach twist.

Finally, I had to put the book down. Closing my eyes, I groaned and rubbed my temples.

"You all right?"

"I hope so."

"Seasick?"

"I guess." I leaned back against the bulkhead and swallowed hard.

"This your first time at sea?" John asked with a sympathetic if slightly amused grimace.

I nodded, clenching my teeth and swallowing hard.

"Go outside," John said. "Stay out on the decks and get some fresh air." His brow furrowed with concern. "Can you make it out there on your own? I can give you a hand if—"

"No, I'm fine." I made a dismissive gesture. My eyes darted toward the box beside his foot. "Stay here. I'll be fine on my own."

He pursed his lips, but then nodded and leaned back against the bulkhead. "If you're gone too long, I'll come after you to make sure you haven't gone overboard."

I laughed. "Thanks."

John was right. The fresh air helped tremendously. Though the afternoon was cool, it wasn't unpleasantly so, and I decided I'd enjoy the nice weather as much as I could before we were knee-deep in the north's bitter cold. I found a spot on the crowded railing and folded my arms over it, letting the crisp, salty air rush across my face and through my hair.

Alternately gazing out at the coast's lush, green scenery and just closing my eyes and enjoying the breeze, I didn't know how long I stood out there. An hour, maybe? Perhaps a little more? Much as I enjoyed John's company and losing myself in a book, the lack of nausea was addictive. I wasn't quite ready to go back down below decks to challenge my stomach again.

Something rustled beside me. I moved over to offer some space and turned my head.

I stiffened.

The well-dressed man peered down his nose at me, scrutinizing me just like he'd scrutinized Ernest and Beatrice's place while he'd looked around the other night. "You're traveling with Dr. Fauth, no?"

Doctor? I swallowed. "I…the man I'm traveling with? I only know his first name."

He scowled. "You don't know who he is?"

Something cold twisted in my gut. "Is there something I should know about him?"

"Well, it isn't wise to travel with a total stranger, now is it?" His tone dripped with condescension. "After all, you should be able to trust your team, shouldn't you?"

I gritted my teeth. "I trust him well enough."

"Good, good." His lips pulled into a grin that made my stomach creep up my throat. "Someone in your...*profession* should be cautious of the company he keeps."

How do you know my profession? I didn't think they'd even noticed me in the brothel, but...

Then the man lowered his voice. "You really don't know what kind of man he is, do you?"

I gulped.

His brow knitted together beneath the brim of his hat. "You should be more careful, son. You never know—"

"What are you talking about?"

He eyed me for a moment. Then he glanced around before dropping his voice to nearly a whisper, so I had to crane my neck to hear him over the other men and the steamboat's engines. "Do you know what's in the box?"

I shook my head.

He laughed dryly. "You're traveling with a man who guards a locked box like a child guards a toy, and you don't even know what's in it?"

Heat rushed into my cheeks. "It didn't seem like it was any of my business."

"Well, it is *my* business. That box he's carrying belongs to me."

I blinked. "I beg your pardon?"

"It contains a device that Dr. Fauth has stolen from me."

They're...colleagues of sorts.

I shifted my weight. "Whatever is in that box is between you and him. I just need to get to Dawson City."

"I see. So you're going with a man who couldn't recruit a team in his own city before coming all the way to Seattle?"

"He's not the first man to come to Seattle alone."

"Yes, but perhaps you should consider why this man in particular came alone." The sinister gleam in his eyes made my skin crawl. "And besides, you know there isn't much gold left in—"

"Everyone knows that." I inched away from him. "I'll take my chances."

"And if you could make more money on this boat than you likely will in the Klondike?"

I rocked back and forth from my heels to the balls of my feet. "What are you talking about?"

"Get me the device." He reached into the inside pocket of his overcoat and withdrew a thicker wad of money than I'd ever seen. "And I'll pay you."

"I'm…" My eyes flicked toward the money again. "I'm not a thief."

"Of course you're not. But Dr. Fauth is. I'm not asking you to steal. I'm asking you to retrieve what's mine."

I drew back a little more. My hip brushed the railing, and I shivered. "How do I know you're not lying?"

"How do you know *he's* not?"

He had a point. But I'd been working in a place where men played cards and drank. I'd seen how quickly disagreements over money and property could escalate, and I'd witnessed too many bloody brawls to think I had any business getting involved in this dispute. Whoever was lying, whoever was the thief, I could be a bad decision away from a bullet to the head.

I took a deep breath and stood as straight as I could. "This is between you and him. I want nothing to do with it."

His dark eyes narrowed. "If you think there's neutral ground in this, think again." He tucked the bills back into his pocket, and then put a heavy hand on my shoulder, making my gut clench. "You be careful whose side you're on."

And then he turned on his heel and walked away. I watched him go, and my knees wouldn't stop shaking. I couldn't forget his comment about someone in my profession. Was John really a thief? Was he dangerous? Was *this* man dangerous?

Being outside may have helped with my seasickness, but I suddenly felt like a deer in wolf-infested woods.

My shaking knees didn't help me walk when the planks beneath my feet kept listing, but in spite of that, I hurried belowdecks. I followed the passageway back to where John and I were staying and threw open the door to our room. As soon as I was safely inside, I shut the door and leaned against it.

"Robert?" John sat up on his rack. "What's wrong? Are you all right?"

I ran a hand through my hair. "I need to know, John. Those men who came into the bar the night we met, are—"

"Did they bother you?" He tossed his book aside and leaped to his feet. "What did they say?"

I cocked my head. "You're not surprised they're here."

He hesitated. "No. I'm not. I...I expected them to try to be on the same vessel. Didn't think they'd bother you, though."

"It was just one of them." I folded my arms across my chest, silently willing my heartbeat to come down. "He asked me about you. And a..." I let my gaze flick toward the half-covered box. "A 'device.'"

"What did you tell him?" The words were so frantic, I half expected John to grab me and shake me.

I narrowed my eyes. "I didn't tell them you were traveling with your own personal whore, if that's what concerns you, though he's obviously well aware of how I've made my living."

Lips parted, John blinked and took a half step back. "I...no, no, that...that wasn't my concern."

"Well, that's all I know about you," I snapped. "So what else could I have told them?"

He dropped his gaze. "I apologize, Robert. I didn't mean to imply anything like that."

"Who are these men, John? I'd like to know before we get out on the open trail if I should be worried."

John swallowed hard. "I suppose I should have been more honest with you before we left."

Oh God. "About?"

He gestured toward the rack where he'd been reading a moment ago. I sat down, and he sat beside me. With his heel, he nudged the box a little farther under the rack, as if to make sure it was still in place. Then he rested his elbows on his knees and clasped his hands together.

I took a breath. "Is it stolen, John?"

"Stolen?" He laughed humorlessly. "Not yet, no."

"What does that mean?"

"It means they"—he waved a hand toward the door—"want to steal it from me."

"Why? What is it?"

John shook his head. "I can't explain it. Not in these close confines."

I gritted my teeth. "I don't know you any more than I know that man. If we're going to travel together, I have to be able to trust you."

"I know. I know." He raked a hand through his hair. "Listen, I can't explain the device. Not here. Only that the men you saw are trying to obtain it for a rival of mine who wants to use it for his own gains."

I glanced at the edge of the box that still stuck out between his leg and mine. "And what gains would those be?"

John started to speak but hesitated. "It doesn't matter. However, I should have told you about these men sooner, and I apologize for that. If you'd..." He paused. "If you'd prefer to go on alone from Ketchikan or ride with another team, I'll understand."

I chewed the inside of my cheek. True, this situation added an element of danger to our travels, but I couldn't go it alone—the mechs required two men to maneuver them, and I couldn't carry my provisions on my own—and thus far, I'd had no luck joining up with other teams. If I joined another in Ketchikan, I wouldn't have the luxury of being choosy about my company. "No, I'd rather stay with you. Assuming I'm right in believing you're not a thief or some kind of fugitive."

John laughed. "No, I'm certainly not." His laughter faded. "But I can't promise anything about those men." He gestured up, as if to indicate my earlier encounter above decks. "My rival is desperate for this device. I don't believe they'd harm us, but they aren't going to give up easily either."

"But you can't tell me what it is?" I eyed the box warily. "I mean, is it dangerous?"

"No, no, of course not. It's..." He paused, then took a deep breath and met my eyes with such intensity I nearly drew back. "I hope you can forgive me if I don't explain what it does. We've only just met, and I..." He dropped his gaze again. "I cannot trust this information with just anyone."

"I understand." And I did. It was only wise for both of us to be wary of each other. "He called you a doctor. What kind of doctor are you?"

"I'm a professor. At a university. And a scientist. I study and build machinery."

That explained his comments about modifying the mech. "He also said you didn't have a team when you arrived because of your reputation in Chicago."

He laughed, shaking his head. "Is that what he said?" He rested his head against the bulkhead and gazed upward. "My, my, Sidney. Your men are getting creative."

"Sidney?"

"Dr. Henry Sidney. My, uh, rival. Another scientist." He met my eyes. "The truth is I came to Seattle alone because there wasn't a man I could trust in Chicago."

"But you can trust a stranger?" *And can I?*

"Anyone I hired in Chicago could've been in cahoots with Sidney. And, well, a stranger can't tell secrets he doesn't know." John put his hand on my knee, the first contact he'd made since leaving my bed. "I mean it, Robert. If you don't feel safe, if you'd prefer to join another team or continue on alone, I'll understand. I'll still pay you as promised, of course, but…I should have warned you about all of this before we left."

I moistened my lips. Half a journey's pay for only getting as far as Ketchikan, and then joining another team for more money? Tempting. Very tempting.

But I liked John. And I hadn't left Montana for an easy journey to the gold fields—the adventure had appealed to my brothers and me as much as the riches that waited.

"Robert? I won't be angry, I swear it. If you want—"

"No." I squared my shoulders. "No, I want to continue with you."

His eyebrows flicked upward. "Are you sure? This could get dangerous."

I grinned. "Well, that'll just make the wealth that much sweeter, won't it?"

He stared at me, disbelief etched across his creased forehead. Then he laughed and patted my knee. "I think you and I are going to get along *quite* well."

Chapter 4

From the Diary of Dr. Jonathon W. Fauth — September 16, 1898

My travels continue to be blessedly smooth, though I expect that to change as I continue into the rugged north. The waters of the Inside Passage are calm, especially to a man who's endured the wrath of the Atlantic, and though the accommodations are anything but lavish, they keep our heads dry and our bellies full enough. Given what's ahead, I shall not complain.

Once we're ashore, we'll be tasked with maneuvering the mech that carries our provisions. The mechs are odd beasts. They are clunky, clumsy contraptions consisting of a wide, flat metal platform with raised sides to hold all our gear. Huge cogs and gears power eight spidery legs designed to—allegedly—claw their way with ease up the icy pass that stands between us and the Klondike. I've not yet had the opportunity to investigate its inner workings, but surely there will be time for that while we camp along the trail.

On either side of the small, boiler-powered engine, two long levers are attached to the mech's front corners, much like reins to a horse's bit, and like reins, they steer the brass creature. It remains to be seen how effectively they'll perform that task when the terrain turns to ice. If this machine survives its journey, I may have to bring it back to Chicago with me. After all, my colleagues would never believe any man would be foolish enough to rely on such a thing, particularly in such conditions. I only hope we can rely on ours all the way to the end of the journey ahead.

I've made reference to 'we' rather than 'I.' This is because my previously singular travels have recently become an accompanied journey. I've written of my plans to acquire a team for the Alaskan and Canadian legs, but those plans have manifested in a most unexpected manner—I expected a team of simpleminded brutes with gold fever, but instead I've hired a young man called Robert. Between us, I expect we'll manage—a larger team would've meant a more heavily laden mech, and I can't imagine the machines are any less clumsy when weighed down.

I encountered Robert by chance in a saloon, and he all but begged to come with me to Dawson City. And for half the going wage, too. Naturally, with the pauper's budget on which I travel, I couldn't pass up a man willing to work for so little. What's unexpected besides his wage is his company. Robert is quite clever. He's usually quiet, content just to listen to those around him or take in his surroundings. I always fear I'll bore someone with scientific babbling, as my brothers call it, but Robert always seems positively spellbound. Small talk and chatter bore him like they do me, but the instant a conversation turns to something with more substance—astronomy, history, the habits of the whales that passed by our vessel this morning—he sits up and leans in close, listening like a man about to learn some invaluable secret. I could easily be spoiled, having such a man with whom to converse.

In his idle time—and my Lord, there is plenty of that on this damned ship—Robert's made judicious use of the books I've brought along. He devours them like I only wish my students would.

Given the arduous journey ahead, I'll consider Robert's company to be a welcome bright spot, something to perhaps temper the misery to come.

In spite of the pleasure of Robert's company and the relative smoothness of my travels thus far, there remains one dark cloud over it all—Sidney's men are relentless in their pursuit. I had—perhaps foolishly—hoped they might lose my trail in Seattle, but they're aboard this vessel. As such, I remain in our quarters as much as I can, leaving only when absolutely necessary and taking the device with me when I do.

We'll arrive in Ketchikan soon, and there I will elude them as best I can. From Ketchikan, the trails branch out in dozens of directions—my only hope is that we choose different paths. Alas, all trails converge on either White Pass or Chilkoot Pass, and even if Sidney's men take White Pass while we take Chilkoot, our paths will converge again in Dawson City.

I only hope we get there first.

L.A. WITT

Chapter 5

From the steamboat, we'd been able to see dry land, but it had been out of reach. I'd nearly begun to believe I'd never set foot on anything besides a boat deck again, but finally, we docked in Ketchikan.

To my surprise, unloading the boat was an efficient process. I supposed the dockworkers had had time to perfect this, but it still amazed me to watch a steady stream of mechs, men, and horses moving onto the dock with little incident. Though some of the horses must not have seen mechs before—at least one spooked, overturning a cart and sending three men onto their backsides in the mud, but no serious injury or damage.

It was strange to be walking on solid, unmoving ground. The mud was thick and sloppy, grabbing on to our boots and our mech's feet, but at least the ground beneath that mud wasn't listing and tilting. The seasickness that had lurked constantly in my gut was finally gone. Even the salty, smoky smells of Ketchikan didn't turn my stomach like the boat's relentless bobbing.

John grinned at me over the mech as we maneuvered it through the clusters of men, mechs, and horses choking the narrow, muddy street. "Feeling better? You look a bit less green."

"Much better, yes. I'm just glad we won't be getting on a boat again anytime soon."

"You're not the only one." He chuckled. "Just be glad you've never gone across an ocean in one. Weeks on end of that madness."

I wrinkled my nose. "I think I'd take my chances with one of those." I gestured at the north end of Ketchikan where a pair of airships hovered over the rows of buildings, their enormous balloon tops swollen and ready to burst. Dozens of ropes were pulled taut to keep the bizarre crafts from floating away.

"They do look awfully tempting, don't they?"

"Better than weeks on end of walking through this." I tugged my boot free from the mud before setting it down in the thick slop again.

"Tempting, yes." John glanced at the airships again, but then shook his head. "Don't know that I'd trust one, myself, though."

I glanced at him. "Why not?"

"If they were reliable, they'd be carrying men all over the world, not just back and forth from this place to Dawson City." He scowled at the pair of crafts. "And at least if a mech breaks down, the worst that happens is we have to repair it or carry our things. One of those breaks down…"

I turned and watched the airships for a moment. The complex systems of engines and propellers were a thing of beauty—I'd seen one in Seattle shortly before it had gone on to Ketchikan—but as with anything, I supposed there was room for failure. And a failed airship was hardly going to just take a knee or limp along like a damaged mech.

We continued through the town, moving at a snail's pace in the thick crowd. There wasn't a room available, but on the outskirts, a vast tent city was growing by the hour. John and I followed the rest of the people and mechs in that direction—at least it gave us an opportunity to learn to maneuver our clunky machine. Every time a horse effortlessly trotted by, whether carrying a man or pulling a cart, I wondered if perhaps we'd bought a con man's junk.

Then I saw a blacksmith shoeing a big gray mare and thought twice. Neither John nor I could shoe a horse, and there'd probably be less and less grass available the farther north we traveled. The mech may have been clumsy and clunky, but it wouldn't throw a shoe or starve to death, and it had spare parts. I'd repaired enough farm equipment, I could hold my own if necessary. John seemed to know his way around machinery too.

And with a little luck, the mech wouldn't break down anyway.

~*~

After we'd set up camp, John began inspecting our mech. He ran his long fingers all over the joints, the rivets, the lines connecting the boiler to the engine. Brow furrowed and lips taut, he inspected every inch of it.

I watched him for a moment. "Something wrong?"

"Not yet, no."

"What does that mean?"

He stood straighter, shaking his head. "This is a terrible design."

"How so?"

"Look at these relief valves." He tapped one with a gloved fingertip. "They're far too small for a device like this." He clicked his tongue. "They either need to be bigger, or there should be more of them."

"So, what does that mean? If they fail?"

"Well, if one of them fails, the others will probably hold temporarily, but they're not designed to cope with that much pressure." He stood, gaze still fixed on the machine. "If two fail, it'll overheat within minutes."

I eyed the mech warily. "And if it overheats…?"

"Best case, it cools down while we repair the valves, and then it runs again. Quite possibly, the coils and tubing melt, and it never runs again." He turned to me. "Worst case, the engine explodes."

I stared at him. "Explodes?"

He nodded.

Shifting my gaze back to the machine, I asked, "Wouldn't we have heard about explosions by now? There've been thousands of these things on the trail."

"There must be a fail-safe in it somewhere. Something that shuts the whole thing down." He tapped the relief valve. "I'd have added a couple more relief valves, myself."

"But, as it's built now…"

John shrugged. "It'll probably be fine, quite honestly. Especially on something this small, I'd say the risk of explosion is only significant if all three valves are disabled, and the boiler has had time to build up enough pressure." He waved a hand. "I just loathe equipment that isn't built to be efficient and sturdy. Particularly with the conditions we'll be facing." He laughed and gestured dismissively. "I'm also not easily pleased when it comes to machinery, so don't lose any sleep over my analysis."

Don't lose any sleep over a boiler that might explode. Of course.

"Anyway, I was going to wander into the town," I said. "Do you want to come with me? This will be our last chance for a proper hot meal for a while."

"And the first one since Seattle." John gestured toward the town. "You go on. I'll stay here. I'd just as soon not leave things unattended."

I almost protested but bit it back. So what if the men had confronted me on the boat? I wasn't going to spend this journey cowering beside John like a child. "Uh, all right. Should I bring anything back for you?"

John thought for a moment, and then shook his head. "No, I think I'll be fine."

While he continued peering at our mech, I trudged through the mud back to the main road through town.

I'd heard that Ketchikan had been a lot like Seattle—just a ramshackle village up until the prospectors had started streaming through. Then buildings had sprung up all along the crowded, muddy streets. Hotels had been built on top of outfitters and saloons.

Pity they didn't have rooms available. No matter, though. We'd have to get used to sleeping in tents and on bedrolls anyway.

I wandered past the shops down by the docks, perusing their bins for anything John or I might find useful. The outfitters had mostly the same things as the ones in Seattle—boots, clothing, coffee, bacon—but priced much higher. One man repaired and sold mechs, but I didn't bother looking at his prices, not even out of curiosity.

The hotels and bars were packed with people, and the smells of baking and frying wafted out into the crowded street. My mouth watered. I hadn't been able to eat much of anything the last few days, and the prospect of freshly baked bread or a—

Oh no.

I stopped dead, nearly sliding in the mud. People said that a few weeks out on the trail made every man look alike—haggard, tired, dirty—but I'd have recognized those three faces anywhere. One in particular.

Heart thumping, I nestled my face into my collar, turned around, and went back the way I'd come. Faster this time. I wanted to break into a run, but that would've drawn attention, so I just kept pace with those who moved briskly through the crowd. I didn't dare look back.

I ducked into an alley, breaking away from the throngs of people, and jogged down the narrow path, boots splashing in puddles. At the other end, I whipped around the corner and—

One of the men grabbed my arm. "Ah, there you are."

The second appeared beside me. "We need to have a talk, son. C'mere."

Before I could shout for help, the second clapped a hand over my mouth, and the two of them pushed me back into the alley.

Where the third, the one who'd spoken to me on the boat, was waiting. "Well. Fancy meeting you here." He stepped toward me. "Have you given my offer any more thought?"

I looked at each man in turn. "Now that you're dragging me into alleys and cornering me, it sounds like more of an order than an offer."

"You're smarter than I thought." He came closer, pushing me back against the wall. The others stood to either side, blocking any chance I had of escaping. "Listen, Robert. We—"

"How do you know my name?"

"I know plenty about you. In fact, them girls at your whorehouse back in Seattle were kind enough to tell us exactly what you did there." He tilted his head toward the end of the alley. "Wouldn't take much to find you a whole new clientele here in Ketchikan."

My blood was colder than the frigid air around us. "I don't even know who you are. Why are you so interested in me?"

"I'm not. You know where my interests lie."

"And I told you I'm not getting involved."

"Robert." He touched my face, the cold leather of his glove caressing my cheek. "You're already involved. And I'm running out of patience."

"Then talk to John," I growled, willing my voice to stay steady. "I have nothing to do—"

"We've discussed this. You've been involved since you joined up with him. Now…" He narrowed his eyes. "I'm done asking. I want my device back, and you *are* going to get it back for me."

"Am I? Or what?"

He trailed a gloved finger down the side of my throat. "Or there's plenty of men in this town who'd pay a pretty penny for a boy like you." His lips peeled back in a grin that sent a sickening chill right through me. "Now, am I going to get my device or not?"

"How do I know it's yours?" I clenched my teeth to keep them from chattering. "How do I know you're not stealing it from him?"

He folded his arms across his broad chest and inclined his head. "I thought you weren't getting involved. Now you're the judge and jury?"

"You're asking me to steal something. I think I have a right to know who the real owner is."

"So you're going to get it for me, yes?"

"I didn't say that."

His lips tightened. I refused to let my fear show, but it was there, coiled tightly around my spine and twisting in my gut.

Then he grabbed my collar and jerked me forward, throwing me off balance. Before I could recover, he spun me around and shoved me face-first against the cold wooden wall. With his knee, he shoved my legs apart. A hand grabbed my testicles so roughly I gasped. I couldn't release that breath. I couldn't think. Couldn't move.

"I want the device back," he snarled in my ear. His grip tightened, bringing tears to my eyes. "Do you understand me?"

I tried to speak, but the air in my lungs refused to move.

"Do you understand?"

"Yes!" I managed to force out the single word and hated that it sounded close to a sob.

One of the other men stepped in. "Let him go, Logan."

My attacker hesitated, but then released me. I dropped to my knees. Immediately, he squatted beside me and jerked my head back by the hair, forcing me to meet his eyes. "I want my device back. Am I clear?"

I nodded as much as his grip would allow.

"When I see you again," he hissed, "I would suggest you have what I'm looking for."

With that, he let go. I fell forward, catching myself before I dropped all the way onto the wet ground. For a moment, I didn't move, just stayed there on my knees with an arm against the wall, shaking and trying to catch my breath as cold mud soaked through my trousers.

What the hell did I do now?

~*~

John was writing in his journal beside the fire when I stumbled back into our campsite. As soon as he saw me, he dropped the journal and stood. "Robert? Are you all right?"

"Those men from the boat." I suppressed a shudder. "They're here."

"Did they—" He looked me up and down, pausing on the mud on my knees, and he paled. "Robert, what did they do to you?"

"Besides letting me know in no uncertain terms what would happen if I didn't bring them your device?"

He cringed, cursing under his breath. "I should've known they'd—"

"What the hell is going on?" I waved a hand toward the town. "These men just cornered me in an alley and threatened to whore me to anyone who'd pay unless I—"

"What?" John's eyes widened. "Are you all right? Did they hurt you?" He reached for me, and I sidestepped him.

"Answer me, John." I pointed at the half-hidden wooden box. "What is in that thing, and why do they want it bad enough that they're willing to threaten me? And damn it, who does it belong to?"

He showed his palms. "It belongs to me, Robert."

"Prove it."

"I—" His eyes darted around our campsite. "I don't dare take it out here. It's…" He shook his head. "I can prove it, but not here."

"Then where?"

"When we're out on the trail, I can—"

"No. I need to know I can trust you before I get out on the trail with you. I…for God's sake, John, who are these men? How long have they been following you?"

John sighed. "I've tried to lose them several times since I left Chicago, but there's no eluding them when they know my destination. And all trails to the Klondike converge at one of two passes, and the trails from the passes converge in Dawson City." He half shrugged. "All I can do is try to stay as far ahead of them as I can."

"I don't suppose you've considered changing your destination."

He eyed me as if I'd lost my mind. "Where else can I go? I need platinum."

"How much are you willing to pay for it?"

"Have you seen the price per ounce of platinum?"

I folded my arms. "Is it greater than your life?"

"My work *is* my life."

I blinked. "John, are you—"

"You're risking your neck to dig for gold. I'm just risking mine for a different metal."

"But I don't—or at least didn't until recently—have someone following me and threatening me." I dropped my hands to my sides. "Look, I knew the journey to the Klondike would be dangerous, but this is *not* what I bargained for."

"No, it's not." John lowered his gaze. After a moment, he met mine again. "I don't want to put you in danger,

Robert. Find another team. I won't leave Ketchikan until you've secured a place with others, and I'll still pay you."

"Can you afford to pay someone who's—"

"I owe it to you."

I searched his eyes. "What about your provisions? The mech?"

"I'll manage it." He gestured at the bustling tent city. "There's plenty of men here. I'll find…I can work something out." Glancing at the mech, he added, "I can't stay here long. I'll hold your gear until you've found a team, but—"

"But hurry. I get it."

He held my gaze, then nodded and extended his hand. "Good luck to you, Robert."

I hesitated, but then shook his hand. "Good luck to you."

Chapter 6

From the Diary of Dr. Jonathon W. Fauth —
September 18, 1898

It appears I'll be continuing my journey on my own. Robert has gone to join another team, and I can't begrudge him that. He came to me last night, badly shaken after another run-in with Sidney's men. I fear they may be more determined than I'd guessed. While finding someone else will be difficult, I can't ask Robert to stay with me at his own peril.

Men in search of teams—and teams in search of men—are in short supply. And going on alone...well, I don't suppose I can. I cannot maneuver the mech alone, nor carry the necessary provisions on my own back. There are horses and mules for sale here. They may be my only option. But what if one breaks a leg? Falls ill? Bolts?

No, I don't dare think about that now. I will find traveling company tomorrow. I must. I have no choice.

Though I'm in haste, I've promised to hold Robert's provisions until he can secure a team. As such, I don't see myself setting out for a day or two. I can't wait long, not with those men nearby, but perhaps the delay will give me time to work out how to elude them. I am seeking alternatives to my original plan of following the trail to Chilkoot Pass. Though I'm unconvinced of their safety and reliability, in desperation I attempted to acquire a ticket for an airship leaving from here in a couple of days. Anything to gain ground ahead of Sidney's men before they're able to obtain my device.

Alas, not even a year's salary could secure me a seat.

There are stories filtering down about terrible weather on the White Pass route, so if I'm unable to find air- or water-based transportation, I may have no choice but to continue as planned. I will venture out in the morning to find a team to join.

Time and again, I wonder if perhaps it was foolish of me to take this journey myself. Surely there is better use of a scientist's time than gallivanting all over this godforsaken countryside in search of a few grains of metal that may or may not be hidden beneath the ice. I am not entirely idle— and I will be walking for many, many hours over the next few weeks before I begin mining—but I am restless nonetheless. I should be working in a lab. Perfecting my devices and racing Tesla and Edison to the semiconductor technology that is just beyond my fingertips.

I cannot reach the Klondike soon enough. And I only hope its ground bears the platinum I so desperately need.

If it doesn't…

Well. I suppose that doesn't bear thinking about, does it?

September 18, 1898 — cont'd

As I lie alone in my tent, I should be able to sleep, but I cannot. Though my body is exhausted, my mind refuses to rest.

The camp is alive with activity at all hours of the night. Men coming and going. Dogs barking. Horses making noise. The feet and engines of mechs.

I've slept through far louder, though. It's nothing but my own paranoia keeping me up tonight. Each time I begin to drift off, I snap awake, certain I'm about to be robbed of the device. At this rate, I'll wake up missing either the device or my mind.

My one comfort is that I am the only one in danger because of this damned contraption. I admit I miss Robert's company—I had looked forward to continuing our conversations out on the trail, but I do not wish to put him in danger.

I haven't seen him since he left. I do hope he's safe and has found a team to take him north.

It's nearly midnight now. I really must sleep.

Chapter 7

My back ached after bedding down on the hard floor of a hotel room with my pack as a pillow. Just as well that I got used to sleeping uncomfortably—there wouldn't be a soft mattress under me anytime soon.

Susan, the prostitute who'd let me sleep on her floor, was still asleep. As quietly as I could, I gathered my things. Before slipping out the door, I left a dollar on her dresser. At least that much she'd be able to keep for herself instead of splitting with the madam. Any whore would've appreciated it just as this one appreciated the warm, safe place to sleep.

Then I hoisted my pack onto my shoulders and made my way out of the brothel and into the already-bustling street.

Arriving in Seattle a lifetime ago, I'd been filled with the excitement of a young man embarking on a great adventure. Standing in Ketchikan, the town as unfamiliar as Seattle was back then, I was instead filled with fear. There was no turning back this time. Even if I didn't want to continue to Dawson City, I had nowhere else to go.

And this time, I was alone.

Alone, and without the naïveté that had made me see adventure, not danger, at every turn. Amazing what a few months could do to a man.

And now, somehow, I had to find another team to get me to Dawson City. Assuming I could find a group whose company was less dangerous than going it alone. Or staying with John. Or giving in to the threats from those three men.

The misty rain gave me an excuse to keep my hat low and my head down, shielding my face. I huddled inside my jacket as I debated what to do next. Where was I supposed to find a team in this town? And what if there weren't any with room on their mechs for my gear? Assuming I still had gear—I'd only taken what I could carry when I'd left John's tent. Though I wasn't convinced John was a thief, I also barely knew him, and I didn't like leaving my provisions in his custody while I sought out another team. But what choice did I have? Without a horse or a mech, I couldn't carry that much gear on my own if I wanted to.

I just hoped I found a team and a mech before John's impatience drove him out of Ketchikan.

There was more competition in Seattle, but there were also more men willing to hire. Here in Ketchikan, teams were already formed. Provisions acquired, tasks assigned. The only teams with room were those who'd lost members along the way, whether from desertion or death. God help me if I needed to do this again in any of the other towns along the way.

I found a few teams who needed more hands, but by noon, I'd had the same conversation at least five times over.

"Where you from?"

"Montana."

"Montana?" Then came the smirk and the slow down-up look. "How'd you even get here, boy? That pack looks like it's heavy enough to flatten you."

"I'm stronger than I look."

The prospector would eye me again, this time like he was sizing up a piece of livestock. Then the inevitable shake of the head. "I'm afraid not. But good luck, son."

Over and over and over.

By late afternoon, I'd all but given up. I was running out of daylight as fast as I was running out of options, and soon, I'd have to find a bed for the night instead of a team for the journey. And if my luck continued like this, I'd have to seek a way to make money before what I had ran out. I'd have plenty once John paid me, assuming he did, but I knew all too well how quickly the coffers could run dry.

I gulped. There was one way I knew to earn money in an outpost town crawling with men who were hundreds if not thousands of miles from home.

No, I wasn't giving up yet. I'd find someone tomorrow. For now, I needed to find food and a bed.

I wandered into a saloon near the docks. Money was in short supply, but I could spare fifteen cents for some whiskey. I found a table near the edge of the barroom, and while I drank, I searched the men in the room, sizing them up as best I could.

I'd seen many of them before. Some had been on the boat from Seattle to Ketchikan. A few had been into Ernest and Beatrice's place. That wasn't a surprise—their saloon was one of the more popular places for travelers to drink, gamble, and fuck before moving on to Alaska.

One caught my eye. I paused for a moment but couldn't remember where I'd seen him. Probably on the boat or around town. I moved on to watching everyone else, but then a memory flashed through my mind, and I shifted my gaze back to him. He was watching me now, eyebrows low over dark eyes as he brought his glass to his lips. His beard was thicker than it had been before, but I recognized him all right.

And he clearly recognized me. My gut clenched as he stood and made his way to where I sat. Without waiting for an invitation, he took a seat in the chair next to mine and, safely under the table where no one else could see, he slid a hand over my thigh. "Thought I recognized you. All the work in Seattle dried up?" He grinned. "Or you headin' north to earn some gold like the rest of us?"

I resisted the urge to shove his hand away. "North. For gold. Yes."

His grin got bigger. "Man like you won't even need to dig." He winked, and I struggled not to shudder. Then he leaned in and lowered his chin and his voice. "You know, I've got half a dozen men sharing two mechs. We're leaving tomorrow for White Pass. Pay's the going rate, but I'll beat whatever your team's paying you as long as you're willing to be discreet." His thumb ran alongside my leg. "Interested?"

I swallowed. The offer got my attention, though the hand on my thigh made my skin crawl. He hadn't been the worst man I'd serviced, not by a mile, but I was desperate to leave that life behind once and for all.

Still, if letting him fuck me meant going north…

"There's room for my provisions?"

"Of course." He subtly kneaded my leg through my trousers. "Plenty of room in the tents too."

"I…" Didn't have many other options. "Where's your team?"

"I'll be right back."

He disappeared into the saloon's crowd for a moment, and when he returned, he had five men with him. He was a large man himself, and the other four dwarfed him. They were hulking men, the kind my grandfather hired in droves to work on the farm. The ones who could nearly double as oxen and draft horses. Shoulders too wide for doorways, arms as big around as my leg.

Plenty of room in the tents. With them. Oh lord.

The one I'd met before stopped and gestured at me. "I've found us some hands for hire."

One of the others folded his arms across his dirty, tattered jacket as he peered down at me. "Little small, ain't he?"

I gritted my teeth.

The first shrugged. "He's made it this far."

The second snorted. "So he managed to not fall off a boat." He shook his head, and as he turned to go, he said, "Good luck, kid."

The first sighed, watching his companions go, and faced me again. "Sorry."

"It's all right." I threw back what was left in my whiskey glass. "Good luck to you and your men."

I got up and started past him, but he caught my arm. "I don't suppose you're available to hire for one night, are you?"

I met his eyes. I barely remembered the night he'd spent in my bed, which meant there hadn't been anything horrible about him. Nothing dangerous or cruel. I shifted my weight. "Will that change my outcome with them?"

He scowled and shook his head. "Once Jack's made his decision…"

Still, it was worth considering. It would take care of where I'd sleep tonight. It would also mean more money in my pocket, which would buy me time to find a team who would hire me. I'd leave my profession behind starting tomorrow, then.

I took a breath, but a booming voice stopped me before I spoke.

"Lars, c'mon." The one called Jack beckoned sharply to my would-be companion.

"Damn." He turned to me and grinned again. "Would've been a pleasant way to spend our last evening before hitting the trail."

I managed a small smile and nodded, and a moment later, he was gone. To my surprise, I was disappointed at the interruption. The arrangement wouldn't have been ideal, but it would have been money and a bed for the night.

Then a thought jolted me. If there was one man here I'd serviced, there could be more. And what about Sidney's men? They knew my face and my profession.

If word got out, there were those who were disgusted to the point of violence by men like me.

Or, worse—those who were *aroused* to the point of violence by men like me.

Suddenly, I felt conspicuous inside the stuffy barroom, almost choking on the air that was thick with musk, sweat, and liquor, and my heart beat faster. I needed to get outside. To breathe.

Once there, I hurried down the street, not sure where I was going, only that I didn't want to stand still. All the while, my mind raced.

As soon as I left Ketchikan, I'd be alone with whichever team I'd joined. Out in the wilderness. At the mercy of men who I had no reason to trust. And after the last few months, I knew all too well how quickly a seemingly decent man could turn into a monster.

A well-dressed gentleman had come to the cardroom one night. He'd been one of the more eccentric visitors to Ernest and Beatrice's saloon, and he hadn't cared one whit if anyone knew he bedded men—he'd asked me to sit beside him at the card table the way the girls often sat with the men they were wooing. He'd teased and flirted, kissing me right on the mouth in front of the visibly uncomfortable gamblers at his table, and more than once he'd hinted about buying me a ticket beside him on the airship he was taking the next morning.

Then he'd retired with me to my room. Beatrice was a harsh madam and rarely let us take nights off, but after that man left, she didn't ask me to work again for a full week.

Anyone in Ketchikan could turn out the same way, and I didn't like these odds—anyone who agreed to hire me might be cruel or turn violent if he found out I'd bedded men, for pay or otherwise.

I slowly turned in the general direction of the tent city. John was the only man in this town who I could predict. Even if he was a thief, I couldn't believe he was dangerous to me. And at least I already knew what kind of man John was with a prostitute. Perhaps not affectionate, but he had a gentle hand. Unless he was extremely adept at keeping his Mr. Hyde beneath the surface, John was not someone to fear, despite the men pursuing him.

On the other hand, although John hadn't touched me since we'd left my room at the brothel, he knew what I was and what I did. Sooner or later…

Still, I was safest with him. And *least* safe with him.

Either way, I didn't see any appealing alternatives.

Nestling my face deeper into my collar, I made my way back to the tent city. I hoped he was still there. He'd promised to hold my provisions until I'd secured a team, but he was a man in a hurry just like everyone here. They didn't call this a gold rush for nothing, and with potentially dangerous men on his tail…

His tent was still there, though, and to my great relief, he was sitting in front of it, writing in his journal beside the fire.

"John?"

When our eyes met, he straightened. "Oh. Robert."

"Hello."

He set aside his journal and stood, tugging at his jacket sleeve. "Ready for your things?"

"Uh. Not quite."

"What?"

I gulped. "Is it…Is it too late to go on with you?"

John's eyebrows rose. "I thought you were worried about the men harassing us."

"I am. But…" I gestured at the box. "Before I agree to it, if that thing is the reason those men are following you—following *us*—I don't think I'm out of place in asking what exactly it is."

"Fair point." John eyed the box briefly. "There are too many ears in this town." I started to protest, but he touched my arm. "When we're a few miles out of town—still close enough to turn back if you're so inclined—I'll explain. But here, in this place…" Shaking his head, he glanced around and shuddered.

"But you'll show me. As soon as we're clear of the town with no one looking over our shoulders."

John hesitated, gnawing his lip, then nodded. "If it'll reassure you enough to stay in my company, then…yes. I will."

"All right."

"What changed your mind?"

"I left because of the men following you. But I have no reason to distrust you." I hesitated, but then met his eyes. "And I have more reason to trust you than I do any other of the men in this place."

John put a hand on my forearm. "You can trust me, Robert. To be honest, I need you for this as much as you need me."

I glanced at his hand. He withdrew it, but the faintest remnant remained of the gentle contact through my thick sleeve. We held each other's gazes, and then John cleared his throat. "We should get some sleep. We'll want to get an early start tomorrow."

"Right. Good idea."

He got up and went into the tent. As soon as I was alone, I released a long breath. Well, I was back where I'd started. The danger of Sidney's men still loomed, and I still didn't know if John was the thief or the potential victim of three thieves.

But strangely, I felt safer than I had since I'd left his tent yesterday.

~*~

I hugged myself inside my thick overcoat, warding off the chill of the drizzly early morning. Beside me, our mech's engine idled quietly, the relief valves hissing and coughing at random intervals, sending little puffs of steam into the air.

The local authorities restricted how many mechs could leave at a time. From what I'd heard, that was something to be thankful for—there were few things that could bring a caravan to a halt faster than a mech bottleneck on a narrow trail, especially if one broke down. With some space between groups, the congestion was minimized.

So for now, we had to wait at the outer edge of Ketchikan with everyone else who wanted to leave.

As we waited, I looked around, searching for three familiar faces within the tired, impatient crowd. I could've sworn I saw the one named Logan earlier, but he'd disappeared too fast for me to be sure.

John kept a close eye on our surroundings as well, drumming his fingers impatiently as he scanned around us. We were boxed in here. That may have been why John kept his pistol on his belt and his overcoat open.

I looked around again, and a face caught my eye. Probably imagining things. God knew I'd thought several times that I'd seen—

No, that was really him.

I swallowed. He was definitely one of the three men. Not Logan, the one who'd threatened me, but he'd been there yesterday. He hung back near some of the other teams, casually smoking a cigar and gazing out at the long line of mechs behind us.

I touched John's elbow. "Over there."

He turned his head, and his whole body tensed. His eyes narrowed and darted back and forth. "See the other two?"

"No."

John pursed his lips. Then he turned so his back was to the man, and gave a slight grin. "I have an idea." He reached into one of our packs and dug around. As he withdrew a folded map, he quietly said, "I'm going to insist we take the White Pass route. You'll argue for the Chilkoot Trail but give in."

"All right."

"Trust me." John turned again so the man watching could see us both in profile. He flattened the map over the top of our provisions and jabbed a finger at one of the painstakingly drawn mountains as he loudly said, "The Chilkoot route is longer and more dangerous. *This* is the faster route."

"What about the weather?" I shook my head. "Between the wind and snow, we'll—"

"Nonsense." John waved his hand. "It's faster, flatter, and the only reason anyone's talking about bad weather is so everyone will go the Chilkoot route and leave the trail less crowded for them."

"And what happens if we get up there and find out the weather really is bad?"

"Then it'll be just as bad on Chilkoot." John folded up the map. "We're taking White Pass."

I glared at him, then put up my hands. "All right, all right. White Pass. But I think we're making a mistake."

He shoved the map into the pack. "And I think you're falling victim to men spreading rumors just to keep the trails clear for themselves."

"Fine." I chanced a surreptitious look at the man who'd been smoking a few paces back. He lingered behind us for a while, then dropped his cigar in the mud and disappeared into the crowd.

"That should do the trick." John stared at the place the man had been standing. "At least until we get to Dawson City."

"Let's hope so."

Chapter 8

The first day of traveling by land was grueling but less so than I expected. The worst was yet to come, of course, so I was thankful for a somewhat easy start. Rain was better than snow, hilly was better than mountainous, and though my feet and back ached by day's end, I wasn't about to complain. Not with hundreds of miles and the arduous task of crossing Chilkoot Pass still ahead before we could claim our riches in the Canadian north.

I could only imagine how I'd feel at the end of one of those days, though, because at the end of this one, I was ready to fall over. While John wrote in his ever-present journal, I warmed my hands by the fire and just enjoyed being off my sore, throbbing feet. At least John seemed equally exhausted, nearly nodding off as he wrote, so I didn't see him asking for anything beyond quiet company by the fire.

And he was good company. As Ketchikan faded behind us and the trail wound into the distance before us, I realized I'd never taken into consideration the abject monotony of walking in the rain along a tree-lined strip of mud.

The mech's *clang-snap-thud*, *clang-snap-thud* steps bordered on maddening. That, and the brass beast wandered more than a distracted horse. Between the noise and the meandering, had I not had John's company, I might have steered the damn thing into a river for spite.

"Pity that by the time the airships are cheap enough for us common men," he'd said this afternoon, gesturing up the trail, "this whole stampede will be over."

I'd looked up at the gray sky, squinting at the rain that stung my cheeks as I trudged through the thick mud. What I wouldn't have given for a leisurely, luxurious passage over the tops of these trees and Chilkoot Pass. "Think they'll be affordable soon?"

"Eventually." John glanced at the sky. "But that's still months, maybe years away. It won't help anyone with Dawson City on his map."

"Pity," I muttered, and kept walking over the wet terrain.

As the day wore on, John told me about his youth as the son of a fur trapper, and how the life in the city had always called to him. The son of a tanner myself, I understood.

"Did your father approve?" I asked.

He laughed. "He'll approve the day I beat Edison or Tesla to something and make a fortune. Until then…" He shrugged. "What about your father? Did he approve of your leaving tanning for Seattle?"

I winced, but John didn't seem to notice. "Well, like yours, he'd probably have approved if my brothers and I had struck it rich. Until I do, the only way I'll regain his favor is to start tanning cowhide with him again." I felt a little guilty lying to John, but he had his secrets too.

John wrinkled his nose. "I'll never understand men like our fathers whose livelihoods involve peeling skin off creatures. Such…grotesque work." He shuddered.

I laughed to myself. From anyone else, I might have taken the comment as snobbery toward those who'd engage in such menial tasks, but John had skinned his share of beasts. That, and he'd loaded the mech and inspected its tools and spare parts as if it had never occurred to him to think such work was beneath him. And having removed the hide of many a cow, I couldn't disagree with his sentiment that it was a grotesque business.

We exchanged glances. Then the mech started wandering again, so I leaned into it while John used the lever on his side to guide it back onto the road.

"Had I more time," he said through gritted teeth, "I'd modify this contraption to navigate itself."

"You could do that?"

"Absolutely."

"I thought you were a scientist. Are you also an inventor or something?"

He shrugged. "An inventor, a scientist, a fool. Depends on who you ask."

"How so?"

"Well," he said, briefly leaning against the errant mech as it tried to veer toward his side of the trail, "I'm researching new technology. Electronic technology. Harnessing electricity to find new ways to make manufacturing more efficient or daily life better. So yes, an inventor and a scientist."

"And they call you a fool?"

He laughed softly, his cheeks coloring. "Every scientist's work is riddled with failure, as is every inventor's. The problem lies in convincing those who've funded all those failures to fund something that will likely also be a failure on the off chance success is just around the next bend."

"Presumably you've been convincing, if they've paid for you to come all this way."

"Yes, well." He sighed. "It was a struggle to persuade them, and if I fail this time, it'll likely be the end of my funding from that or any other university."

"Then I certainly hope you find enough in Dawson to convince them to continue funding you," I said. "Though with that much gold, you might not need their funding."

"Oh, as I said before, I'm not interested in gold." He paused. "Well, no more than the next man, I suppose. I may be a fool to some, but I wouldn't turn away a bag of gold."

"Oh, yes. Platinum. I'd forgotten." I glanced at him. "But, why a gold stampede?"

"Platinum is extremely difficult to find. Very, very rare. But where there's gold, more often than not, there's also platinum. Trace deposits, really, but I don't need much to start with. It's invaluable to my work, so it's worth the journey."

"I've heard the fields are enormous, though," I said. "You expect to find traces of anything in a place like that?"

John looked my way, and his grin reminded me of a devious child's. "This is why I have that device that Sidney's men so covet. Let's just say it'll make my needle easier to find in the haystack." He gestured at the locked box tucked in amongst our provisions. Lowering his voice to nearly a whisper, he said, "I'll show you when we reach the fields." His eyes darted ahead of us, then behind us, before meeting mine again. "No one can know about it who doesn't already, or every man will be out to steal it."

I nodded but said nothing. I didn't begrudge him his secrecy anymore, especially with those men hunting him.

Shortly before nightfall, we stopped. Tents and tied horses lined the edge of the trail as far as I could see in both directions, though a stubborn few kept going, probably hoping to gain a few more miles before bedding down for the night. I didn't envy them trying to put up a tent in the dark—the daylight alone was worth stopping now.

We set up the tent beside the mech. After John chained the mech's legs to a tree so it wouldn't be stolen, we moved the most valuable of our provisions into the tent. Coal, weapons, some food—the things we didn't dare risk losing. He tucked the mysterious box in the corner of the tent, near where we'd laid out our bedrolls. Everything else would have to weather the elements and hopefully not wind up in the possession of passing thieves.

"Robert." John gestured for me to come into the tent with him.

I froze. He didn't want...out here? When it was this cold?

Damn it. We'd never discussed those terms. I'd foolishly never established that I wanted to be here as a fellow prospector, not as a prostitute.

He glanced back, eyebrows up. "Something wrong?"

"Uh...No. Nothing's wrong."

With my heart in my throat—*not now, John, please*—I followed him into the tent.

Our bedrolls had been laid out, and I almost instinctively reached up to take off my jacket but stopped when I saw the mysterious locked box in the middle of his bedroll.

He knelt beside it and fished a key from his pocket. "I promised you proof. I hope you'll forgive me if I keep the device itself under wraps, but..."

Now I felt like a fool, but a relieved fool. I knelt beside him.

He opened the padlock and lifted the box's lid. Something about the size of my forearm was covered with dark velvet, and he pulled some folded papers out from under it. Drawings and such. Then he handed me the first page. "I hope this is sufficient."

I took the page. Most of the writing consisted of numbers and diagrams that made no sense to me.

"At the bottom," John said softly. "That should put your mind at ease over who has stolen from whom."

I looked at the bottom.

United States Patent Office.

Patent Pending – To be issued to Fauth, Jonathon William.

Exhaling, I handed it back. "So it is yours."

He nodded. "Forgive me for not going into detail about its function, but—"

"It's all right. I just wanted to know for sure it was yours."

He put the device away and we went back outside.

As we sat in silence beside the fire, John's pen scratched quietly across paper, and occasionally, he'd pause to stare into the campfire or up at the night sky, his eyes unfocused and brow furrowed, before he'd resume writing.

All the while, in the back of my mind, I thought about how I'd felt when he'd summoned me into the tent. The device hadn't even crossed my mind. I'd been certain he'd had other intentions, and now I dreaded crawling into the tent to bed down for the night. In my haste to get out of Seattle, and of Ketchikan, I'd agreed to John's terms without first making sure we were clear on *all* the terms. Certain terms had crossed my mind, but it hadn't occurred to me I might not be as agreeable to them by the time we'd made it this far.

I was a prostitute. When a prostitute was paid, certain services were expected. Even if we hadn't discussed such a thing before I'd set off with him on this journey, he was paying me, I was a whore, and I'd have been foolish to be surprised if—when—he finally decided it was time for me to earn my keep.

That time could very well come tonight. A knot formed in my gut. There hadn't been privacy aboard the boat, so the point had been moot, and I suspected John had been too nervous about Sidney's men to think of anything else.

But now we'd be sleeping side by side in a cramped tent with no prying eyes. He didn't have to fear discovery as long as we both remained quiet.

Stealing a glance at him in the firelight, I swallowed hard. He was attractive beyond words, and I liked him, but I was exhausted. More so than I'd ever been in my life. My body ached, my feet hurt, my eyes barely stayed open. Much as I'd enjoyed the night I'd spent with him, if I so much as saw a cock just now, I'd collapse into tears. I was too damned *tired*.

But I'd do whatever I had to do to continue with John. The farther we traveled, the less I could risk being alone in bandit-infested country with only my pistol and what little I could carry. If John required me to earn my pay, then I would, but dear Lord, I didn't know where I'd find the energy tonight.

To be on the safe side, though, I'd gone into the tent earlier under the pretense of putting something into my pack. I'd withdrawn the opaque glass bottle from my pack and slipped it beneath the fur blanket along with the socks and shirt I'd wear tomorrow. If I had to please him tonight, at least I could have warm lubricant.

John closed his journal, and my heart thundered in my chest. With a nod, he indicated the tent. I gulped and rose, dreading where the night would take us.

I doused the fire, and John checked for the hundredth time that his locked wooden box was safely stowed in a corner of the tent.

Neither of us spoke. We both took off our boots and coats. The weather was chilly, but not yet cold enough to necessitate sleeping in *every* stitch of clothing we owned. Much as I disliked bitter cold, it would have given me an excuse to keep as many layers as I could between John and me.

I lay back on my bedroll and pulled the thick fur up to my nose. The blanket was big enough for both of us, and despite the warmth, I shivered beneath it, unsure of how to feel about being under the same covers as him. Staring at the top of the tent, I held my breath, listening to him move around as he got under the fur just inches from me.

Exhaustion made the thought of coupling unbearable, and I was scared to death that he was a heartbeat away from asking me to undress. With every rustle and movement, I was sure his hand or body would find mine.

But then he was still. Before long, his breathing slowed, and soon, he was snoring softly beside me. I released my breath. He must have been as tired as I was.

Maybe another night, he'd demand his money's worth, but not tonight.

With my worries assuaged, I drifted off beside him.

~*~

For days on end, we talked by day, slept by night, and never touched.

The cold hadn't really set in yet, though. When it did, any man who wanted to survive the night would huddle against anyone within reach, and I dreaded that night.

It came a little over a week after we'd left Ketchikan. The sky was clear and it was too cold for snow to fall on the frozen ground anyway. There was no way we were sleeping apart tonight, but perhaps it would be too cold for him to ask anything of me beyond body heat.

After we'd set up camp, John took a peculiar device out of the stack of provisions. It was a brass box with three coils inside, and when he removed a glowing coal from the mech's boiler and put it into a small compartment of the little box, not ten minutes later, those coils glowed like the coal had.

He set it near the side of the tent, careful to keep it from touching the material so it wouldn't catch fire, and tucked a thin pipe under the edge of the tent. "It'll blow the exhaust outside. Otherwise, we might be warm, but we'd be too dead to enjoy it."

I was wary of the little device, but when the air inside the tent warmed, I decided it was well worth the risk of burning or poisoning us. As I settled onto my bedroll, I was toastier than I'd been since the last time I'd slept in Beatrice's brothel.

John pulled the fur up over himself on his own bedroll. The little device hummed and gurgled, but otherwise, our tent was silent. And it stayed that way.

Though my bones ached with exhaustion, I lay awake listening to his breathing and his machine. The conditions were certainly inviting. We were tired, of course, but that hadn't stopped many of the men who'd celebrated their return from the Yukon with a visit to a whore's bed.

I turned my head. The faint sunset-colored glow of the heater illuminated John's shape, picking out the rise of his shoulder beneath the thick fur and a few tendrils of his hair. He was sound asleep—when had I memorized the way he breathed?—and as much as I'd dreaded having to earn my pay for this journey, I caught myself feeling a little disappointed that he hadn't asked me to.

"Do you like that, Robert?"

I swallowed, shifting my gaze back to the top of the tent. I didn't remember anyone else ever asking me that before. Certainly not because they wanted to know the answer. And maybe John hadn't cared. Maybe it had just been something to arouse his ego, to convince himself he was as good as most men who fucked me thought they were, but as I heard the words over and over in my mind, I couldn't make myself believe that.

And the fact was, I *had* liked it. I never wanted to be any man's whore again as long as I lived, but I was only lying to myself when I said I didn't want John's touch.

But he didn't touch me.

He just slept.

~*~

The next morning, as he packed away the device, he said, "We'll have to use it sparingly. We could burn through half a bag of coal in that thing before we're anywhere near the

Yukon, so it's only for nights when the cold is truly unbearable." He glanced around the trail. "Like my other device, no one can know about this. As the weather gets worse, men will be willing to cut our throats for this kind of heat."

I gulped. I'd shivered my way through twenty winters in Montana. After a night of sleeping in that wonderful warmth, I could imagine how desperate everyone would be for the same once that deep, unavoidable cold set in. "I won't say a word."

He smiled. "I know. Now let's get moving. How are your feet?"

"Sore and cold, but I'll manage." I chuckled. "Guess we'll both have to get used to that, won't we?"

John laughed. "Well, you probably have the advantage over me after growing up where you did." He held up his gloved hands. "My fingers are good and callused from my work, but I can't say the same about my feet."

"Except I haven't been on a farm in a while."

"Oh. Well. No, I suppose you haven't. But your profession has had you on your feet more than mine."

I blinked.

His cheeks darkened. He cleared his throat. "The bartending portion, I meant."

"Right. Right." I muffled a cough. "So, we should get moving, right?"

"Yes, we should." He tugged at one of his gloves. "Ready?"

"When you are."

We were well out of Ketchikan by then. The trail was virtually deserted in places, the crowd having thinned along the way as mechs broke down, horses rested, and men stopped at trading posts and native villages. In Skagway and Juneau, many groups stopped to rest. From there, dozens had branched out onto different roads and trails which promised to bypass some of the steeper terrain or get them to Chilkoot Pass faster. Since the end of the first week, it hadn't been unusual for us to be alone for hours at a stretch before we passed another party or someone passed us.

Whether we were amongst others or walking alone, John and I continued our conversations, which meandered like the path beneath our feet and the mech that staggered between us. We talked about our families and their disappointments when we'd gone off to pursue our unusual dreams. He told me about some of his eccentric colleagues and impossible-to-please superiors. With the help of a little whiskey from John's flask, I told him about some of the bizarre things I'd seen and heard during my time as a prostitute. He couldn't quite believe I'd really spent not one but three nights with the son of the owner of one of the major logging companies, and I insisted he was telling tales when he said one of his former lovers had left Chicago—and him—to take a seat in the Senate in Washington, DC.

And still, when the cold nights came, the conversations faded and we slept apart.

Chapter 9

From the Diary of Dr. Jonathon W. Fauth —
September 23, 1898

I've been remiss in writing since our arrival in Alaska.

We are now en route to Chilkoot Pass. I have never known such exhaustion in all my years, and I'm certain my boots will be worn to my socks in a matter of days. Even now, as I write beside our campfire, my eyes grow heavy, so forgive me if this entry lacks coherency.

My faith in our mech wanes with each passing hour. After inspecting the contraption more closely, I worry that we've fallen prey to the outfitters' attempts to get rich off those with gold fever. Our mech appears sturdy, powered by a small but efficient steam-powered device, but the construction of the legs has left me unimpressed.

Then there's the engine—I've spent most of the day trying to come up with a better design for the inadequate relief valve system, but implementing such a thing out here may prove difficult if it's possible at all. I can only be vigilant and check the valves frequently to make certain they're working properly.

Now I see where the stories of mechs falling down the Chilkoot or getting stuck in holes have originated—poorly designed machinery on an already-treacherous trail. The metal is thin in places it ought to be reinforced, and though the joints are well made, are they suited for the weight they're being asked to carry over rugged, frozen terrain? I'm not convinced.

Fellow passengers and men camping in Ketchikan with us were filled with stories of heaps of mangled mechs at the base of Chilkoot Pass, and the skeletal remains of the same scattered along the trails. They're susceptible to ice, malfunction, vandalism—and that's assuming they don't go errant and fall down ravines.

Like vultures, men descend upon the disabled mechs, stripping them down to their brass skeletons. Cogs, springs, entire legs, even nuts and bolts, anything that can be is salvaged, rendering the already-crippled machines useless.

Barring a disastrous malfunction, though—particularly from those damned relief valves—I believe I can keep the beast on its feet until we're over the Chilkoot Pass and into Canada. From there, if it's as troublesome as I predict, we'll abandon it, take what we can carry, continue on foot, and sort out return transportation when we reach Dawson City. It is imperative I get to the gold fields as soon as possible and obtain as much platinum as it may yield. Pity we haven't the money for an airship ticket—we'd be in Dawson City in no time, and we'd easily elude Dr. Sidney's men.

At least we don't have to rely on pack animals. No amount of inventing and tinkering will put a horse's leg back together.

The mech came with two bags of coal, and we've been warned to use it sparingly. Water for the steam is as easy to find as stooping to pick up some snow, but the coal must last us all the way to Dawson City and back. If we run out, wood will suffice as a substitute, but it isn't nearly as efficient, especially when most of the timber out there is wet or frozen. I shall heed that advice and guard our coal as jealously as I guard my device.

It is more than a little tempting, I promise you, to ride on the mech like it's a coach. Walking the next four hundred miles to Chilkoot Pass, and the subsequent couple hundred across the Yukon, is hardly appealing, is it? The machine can easily bear our combined weight in addition to our ridiculous amount of gear and provisions, but every outfitter emphatically warns prospectors to stay off the mechs. Some fools still ride them, I understand, reasoning they should save their energy for walking up the passes. But all it takes is a particularly bad patch of ice or a badly placed rock, and the stampeder suddenly has to worry less about saving energy and more about how to cart himself over the pass with a busted leg. I'm told a few dozen learned this lesson the hard way, and now most everyone walks beside the brass spiders.

After a few miles of constant nudges, Robert and I have both quite bruised our hips, but then Robert fastened a couple of unused pairs of mittens to the corners for padding. I told you he was clever!

There's been no sign of Sidney's men since we left Ketchikan, so I believe they've fallen for our deception and gone toward White Pass instead of Chilkoot Pass. Still, I remain vigilant. They will not hinder my journey, nor will they interfere with my platinum acquisition. Not while I still have a chance at beating Sidney, Edison, and Tesla to creating this new technology.

For tonight, though, I can no longer ignore this fatigue. I need to check once again that the device is safely hidden in the tent, douse this campfire, and sleep.

Chapter 10

The wind and rain were getting colder by the day. Even though it was only September, it wouldn't be long before the rain pelting my face would be tiny crystals of ice, and the snow wouldn't be far behind. At least the trail would stay mostly clear—thousands of stampeders before us had carved a wide, muddy road through the wilderness. If it snowed during the night, though, we'd have to maneuver the damned mech through it.

On the bright side, I had someone to talk to. Many of the teams seemed to trudge along in silence, but John and I nearly always found something to discuss.

"So you came to Seattle with your brothers," he said on the trail one frigid morning, pausing to nudge the wandering mech with his hip. Once it was back on its correct path, he glanced at me. "Where did your brothers go? Are they still in Seattle?"

I hesitated. Shame twisted beneath my ribs at the thought of my brothers. "One, I don't know. The other, uh, went back to Montana. Gone to work for our father."

John glanced at me over the mounds of gear on the mech. "And I can't imagine you want to go back to that."

"I didn't exactly dream of the life I had in Seattle, but I wasn't ready to give up on the rest of the world in exchange for a life of tanning cowhide."

"Is that why you can't go back?"

It was easier than the truth, so I just nodded.

"If I may ask," he said softly, "what happened to the provision money you and your brothers brought with you?"

I sighed. "My brother loved whores, but I lost plenty of it on a card table too." My cheeks burned. "I had hoped to secure us better traveling conditions, maybe even an airship, but by the time I was done and my brother had slept in every bed in Seattle, we couldn't even afford to go back to Montana." Well, that much was true, anyway.

"I can't blame you for trying to secure better travel." John pursed his lips. "I looked into alternatives myself, but the university wasn't about to pay those prices. If I want to dig, they told me, they'd get me to Seattle by train, and I was going the rest of the way on foot."

"And here you are."

He laughed. "Here I am."

And I thanked God that he'd let the subject drop.

~*~

A few hours later, as we rested our exhausted legs beside the campfire, I couldn't ignore the wooden box half-covered by a flour sack between us.

"So, uh. I'm curious about the device."

John stiffened. "What about it?"

"The men who are following you—do they know what it does? Obviously they know it exists, but do they know its function?"

John sighed and gazed into the fire. "Unfortunately, yes. A few months ago, some of my notes were stolen."

"Notes about the device?"

"Yes. Not enough to build one, but enough to understand its purpose."

"Do you know who they are? The men following us, I mean?"

John nodded slowly. "They work for Sidney. As I said before, he's a competitor of mine. We're both involved in producing electronic devices using semiconductors. He's been using any means necessary to try to get his hands on the plans or the prototype. Or both."

"I didn't realize scientists were so…cutthroat."

He laughed. "All's fair in love and war, and believe me, when you're competing with Edison and Tesla, it is most certainly war." He absently tugged at his glove. "My lab's been broken into three times in the last six months, and now Sidney's got his men following me all the way out here."

My stomach flipped. "What lengths do you think they'll go in order to get it? I mean…" When he looked at me, I raised my eyebrows, unsure how to word the rest of the question without sounding like a coward.

John dropped his gaze. "I don't know. I had hoped to lose them in Seattle, but they're determined if they've followed me as far as Ketchikan." He met my eyes again. "Hopefully we've thrown them off and sent them toward White Pass, but they'll be in Dawson City sooner or later. And, well, it still isn't too late to join another team if you're worried. I don't know how determined they are. I don't know what lengths they'll go to for the device. To be quite honest, I can't promise you're safe with me."

I gulped. "Is anyone safe on this trail?"

He studied me. "No reason to increase the danger, is there?"

I considered my options for a moment, but there weren't many of them. "I'll take my chances with you. May I, um, may I see it?" I gestured at the mostly deserted trail. "Since there's no one here?"

John's lips quirked, and he looked up and down the trail. "All right. I suppose there's no reason to hide it from you now."

My heart quickened. I had been curious but hadn't actually expected him to show it to me. Without a word, I followed him into the tent, and he lit a small lantern so we could see without leaving the tent flap open.

He unlocked the box.

Inside, a half-dozen corked vials of some sort of liquid were nestled into padded slots along one side. Across the inside of the lid, thin strips of material held a row of fine tools and instruments in place. In the middle, an object about the size and shape of my forearm was wrapped in deep-crimson fabric.

John glanced back at the flap, and then lifted the velvet cover and pulled out the device.

I leaned in closer to see. The device was brass, not unlike the mech parked outside. Coils lined one side, opposite the leather-wrapped handle that John gripped. On one end was a liquid-filled glass bubble at the top, and at the other, what appeared to be a miniature boiler like the one on the back of the mech, only much tinier.

As I turned to him, I said, "How does it—"

And suddenly we were face-to-face. So close I could feel his body heat.

I moistened my lips. "How does it work?"

John swallowed. Then he turned his attention back to the device. "It's, uh, it detects noble metals in the soil. Using an electrical charge." He pointed at a complex network of metal and wires at the heart of the device. "It identifies the conductivity and a few other characteristics of metals within the soil. If it registers certain levels, indicating the presence of noble metals, then that's where I'll dig."

"And you'll find platinum?"

"Most likely. There are other noble metals. Gold, of course. But where there's gold, there's frequently veins of platinum." He faced me again, meeting my eyes from not very far away. "We can work together in the gold fields. With any luck, we'll both find what we're looking for."

I raised my eyebrows. "So it…it does find gold?"

John searched my eyes for a moment, then nodded. "If we're in a gold field, and the device finds noble metals, odds are it'll either be gold or platinum. Quite likely both."

I held his gaze. "Think we'll find it?"

John swallowed. "I don't know."

We locked eyes for a long moment, but then John cleared his throat and looked at the device. "So, I hope it's clear now why I've been so secretive over this device. If word gets out…"

"I understand. Your secret's safe with me."

Once again, he met my eyes. "Thank you, Robert."

~*~

As we sat on the mech beside the river and ate another agonizingly bland meal of half-cooked beans the next morning, I broke the silence. "You haven't said much about a family back home."

"There isn't much to tell. My parents are still living, and my brothers aren't far from them, but I rarely see them. We write letters, but…" He shook his head and picked at the beans in his bowl.

"Do they live far away?"

"Not really." He laughed, but it was a sad sound. "To be honest, I'm usually so caught up in my work, I barely leave the lab, let alone the city. And my mother is terrified of Chicago." His gaze darted toward me. "What about you? Do you send letters to your family?"

I shook my head. "I've sent a couple of telegrams, but…"

He watched me for a moment. "You seem very lonely, Robert."

The words hit me in the chest. "So do you."

He winced. "Yes, I suppose I am. My work doesn't really allow for companionship, though."

"Is it worth it?"

He furrowed his brow. "What do you mean?"

"Your work. Is it worth the lack of companionship?"

He lowered his gaze. "If I could have both, I would, but the work I do requires sacrifice." He lifted one shoulder in a taut half shrug. "And a man like me isn't much of a companion for someone who needs one."

"How so?"

"I'm in my lab for hours on end. Sometimes days." John's lips tightened. Then he sighed. "I suppose I can't fault my last lover for leaving." He idly scraped his empty bowl with the edge of his spoon as he looked out at the forest. "Maybe I was too focused on my work. I was so close to a working prototype, I could feel it, but…" He tapped the heel of his boot against the mech's leg. "So many late nights in the lab, and all the secrecy about us. It must have killed him to not only have to be my secret, but to see so little of me that there was hardly enough going on to cause a scandal in the first place. I can't begrudge him leaving. He had his own ambitions, after all. Political and whatnot. It just…" He trailed off. Then, all at once, he came to life and turned to me. "What about you?"

"Hmm?"

"Ever had someone like that?"

"Me? No." I laughed quietly. "Not a great surplus of willing men in a town like mine, and I've hardly presented myself as much of a suitor since I've been in Seattle."

"Did you have anyone before…before your time in Seattle?"

I chewed the inside of my cheek. I couldn't say I was ashamed of what I did any more than I could say I was proud of it, but I loathed admitting the only time I'd ever felt a man's touch had been when I'd been paid for it.

"Robert?"

I cleared my throat and hoisted myself off the mech and onto the muddy grass. "We should get moving. There isn't much daylight left."

He watched me silently but let the subject drop. The question lingered in his eyes, though, and occasionally appeared on his face as a crease of gentle inquisitiveness.

But he didn't ask.

Not until we'd stopped for the night, anyway. As we sat beside the fire with our supper, he set his bowl aside, the spoon clinking against the edge. "Let me ask you something."

"All right."

"You were in Seattle for a while, yes?"

I nodded.

"And you weren't at all surprised when your employer and I were discussing the rumors that there's no gold left in the Klondike. You know this is going to be a miserable journey, and likely one with few rewards." He studied me, the fire's reflection flickering in his eyes. "If you can afford the journey to Dawson City, why not spend the money to go back to Montana?"

I stared into my mostly empty bowl. "I can't go back."

"Forgive my curiosity," he said, his voice gentle and soft, "but why can't you go back?"

I took a deep breath and set my bowl on the ground beside me. "The thing is, my father loaned the three of us money to go to Dawson City. When we made it to Seattle, we..." I sighed and shook my head. "Turn three boys loose in a city like that with more money in their pockets than they've ever seen, and—"

"And it's not going to end well." He chuckled softly, but his expression remained sympathetic.

"It didn't." I held out my hands for the fire to warm. "My elder brother, he discovered the whores. And I..." Heat rushed into my cheeks, and it had nothing to do with the flames in front of me.

"You...what?"

I swallowed. "I discovered cardrooms."

"Poker?"

I nodded. "Between us, we lost most of it. When we realized we couldn't afford to go north or go home, we panicked. We did whatever we could to recover the money. Sold things. Went to work for anyone who would hire us. That's…how I ended up working for Ernest and Beatrice." I hesitated, then met his eyes. "As a whore."

He held my gaze, and though I kept expecting to see judgment in his face, he offered none. Curiosity, if anything. After a moment, he sipped from his mug and then set it down beside the bowl. "With all the outfitters in Seattle, all the entrepreneurs, that was the only way you could earn your—"

"I did what I could," I snapped.

John put up a hand. "I understand, Robert. I do. I just can't imagine there was no other means for a man of your intellect to—"

"Intellect is no cure for desperation."

He regarded me silently, then gave a slow nod. "I suppose that's true. I'm sorry." He paused. "Where are your brothers now?"

"I don't know where George is. That's my elder brother. As for Paul…" I gritted my teeth. "He was angry with us, and I suppose he had every right to be." I shook my head again, wishing there was something a lot stronger than campsite coffee in my tin mug. "He didn't like me working in the brothel but couldn't argue with the money. And he and George were making money too, so it looked like we might have enough to get to Dawson City after all." I swallowed some coffee. "Then we found out George was trying to win back some of the money in the cardrooms. And he was winning, but since that was how we'd lost so much in the first place, Paul got angry with him. I came back from the brothel one morning to find George still drunk and Paul gone with what was left of the money."

John's eyebrows rose. "He just...left?"

I nodded. "A few weeks later, our father sent us a telegram. Paul had gone home, and he'd told him everything." I lowered my gaze again, staring at the ground between my feet. "*Everything.*"

For a long time, the only sound was the crackling fire. A spark popped, and the sound seemed to echo for miles.

"So when you say you can't go home to Montana," John said after a while, "you really can't."

Still staring at the ground, I nodded again.

"You know, there's no shame in doing what you had to do to survive."

I laughed bitterly. "Explain that to my father. He won't have a gambler or a fornicator under his roof, and he certainly won't have a son who's been a prostitute."

"Then he's a fool." The vehemence in John's voice startled me. He put a hand on my knee, sending a shiver straight up my spine. "You're a good man, Robert. You've made your mistakes, but you're a good man."

"Thank you." I clung to my coffee cup to keep from putting my hand on top of his. "And by the way, thank you again. For hiring me. Both times."

"Thank you for accompanying me." An odd smile played at John's lips. "Both times."

I laughed softly, and the way our eyes met made my heart race. I quickly looked away and picked up my empty bowl. "I suppose we should turn in."

"Yes, we should."

He took his hand off my leg, and damn, I wished he'd put it back.

.

Chapter 11

On the morning of the fifteenth day, our forward progress ground to a halt in a huff of steam and a screech of twisting metal. One of the steam lines blew, which knocked the mech off balance mid-step and caused it to land just right to mangle the front-most left leg.

With the help of two other teams, we managed to move the mech off the trail so people could continue past us. Once we were out of the way, we both glared at the crippled spider, then looked at each other.

"What happened?" I asked.

"Damn relief valves." He gestured at the machine. "Looks like condensation froze one of them shut and over-pressurized the boiler. "We're lucky, though. It could have been much worse."

"At least it didn't explode."

"Exactly." He knelt beside the mech and inspected the damage. "Well, we're not moving anytime soon." He pulled off his heavy gloves and took a thinner leather pair from his jacket. As he put them on, he said, "Would you grab the bag of tools and spare parts, please?"

The ruptured line turned out to be tucked too far under the back of the mech for both of us to work on. It was certainly more his expertise than mine anyhow, so I was idle for the moment. I leaned against the mech, arms folded on top of its raised side, while he knelt on the ground on a flour sack.

Frowning over the ruptured line, John said, "So, what will you do after all of this?" He glanced up, smirking. "Assuming this beast walks again."

"I suppose it depends on whether or not I strike it rich."

"And if you do?"

I shrugged. "Don't know. Maybe go east. See what kind of life I can make. Maybe in New York."

John gestured sharply with a wrench. "Bah, you don't want to go to New York."

"Chicago's better?"

"God no." He furrowed his brow and cursed at a stubborn piece, but it finally came free. As he set it on the ground beside him, he said, "New York and Chicago are much the same, except there's more wind in Chicago. You don't want to go there either."

"But that's where you're going, isn't it?"

"I don't intend to strike it rich in Dawson City." He glanced up at me with a knowing grin on his lips. "If I find what I'm looking for, I'll return to Chicago, and then, my friend, I'll strike it richer than any man who's put pickax to soil in the Klondike."

"And if you don't find the platinum?"

"If I don't find it, I…" His brow creased. Then he sighed, shrugged, and started on the line again. "Then I'll go back to Chicago and hope I can continue my work."

"Why wouldn't you be able to continue?"

"Because the university will only pay for a finite amount of speculation and tinkering, as they so eloquently call it." He frowned again, though I couldn't be sure if it was directed at his thought or the steam line. "This attempt to get enough platinum to complete my work is the last time they'll indulge me, and if I fail, there won't be any more money or lab space. As it is, even if I don't fail, the university is threatening to send my funding to Tesla so they can get in on his discoveries." John snorted and shook his head. "Damn fools. They think I'm delusional, but somehow *his* creations are genius."

"And finding platinum will convince them otherwise?"

"Well…" He paused to secure the new line into place. "I need the platinum for the semiconductors I'm working with. Hopefully *those* will convince them."

"The what?"

"Small electrical parts." He pushed himself to his feet, grimacing as he gingerly rubbed his lower back. "Once I have the metal I need, I can make those with relative efficiency, and then I can make more progress with the rest of my work."

"Which is…?"

He smiled. "I'm working on some advances that could revolutionize the way cities communicate."

"A better telegraph?"

"Beyond a telegraph, my friend." He beamed. "Being able to speak across the lines, not only hear each other but even *see* another's face." He gestured at his own face, then laughed and shook his head. "All I have to do is beat Edison and Tesla to it."

"Well, I don't think I've seen them come through town, so…" I grinned.

He laughed. "Oh, they're occupied with other nonsense. They think I'm as crazy as the university does. I mean, who could possibly need to make enough semiconductors to require as much platinum as I do?" He clicked his tongue. "Well, we'll just see when I finish, won't we?"

"So we will." I didn't know anything about that kind of thing, so I took him at his word that he really was on the cusp of something great. I couldn't imagine being able to hear someone's voice from miles away. Seeing their faces? How absurd.

I shifted my weight and rested my chin on my arms. "So how do you *know* there's platinum in the Klondike?"

"I don't. But they've found gold there." He shrugged. "I've been to three other gold digs, and I've found it there every time."

"So you've already found it." I tilted my head. "Why go to the trouble to find it again?"

"Because I didn't find enough. I only need a small amount for the prototypes, but to manufacture additional machines in enough numbers to make an invention useful? That's why I'm wandering all over the world to gold fields in hopes of finding a decent deposit."

"Where else have you done this?" I gestured toward the trail. "Made the journey to gold fields, I mean."

"Most recently, South Africa. I acquired a sufficient cache there, actually. Enough to finish the prototypes and possibly manufacture a few more." He scowled. "But I was robbed in London before I came back to Chicago. Haven't found such an amount since then." He glanced toward the north as he wiped his hands on his trousers and released a wistful sigh. "The university is losing patience, believe me. They think I'm just a reckless miner masquerading as a professor and scientist." He was quiet for a moment before turning to me. "What about you? What will you do if you leave Dawson City empty-handed?"

"I'm not certain. I've already found one way to survive if I need to."

His lips tightened as he searched through a bag of parts. "You can't do that forever, though."

"No, but I can do it until I figure out what else there is for a man like me."

John pulled a new line and a brass coupling out of the bag. "And what kind of man is a man like you?"

"Don't know." I let my own gaze drift toward the north and the not-yet-visible Klondike gold fields. "I'm hoping to figure that out before this is all over."

"Yes, I suppose a journey like this could tell a man a great deal about himself."

"One can hope."

By midafternoon, the boiler was working again and, with a large rock, a long tree limb, and a lot of cursing, we'd straightened the bent leg. The only problem was…it was midafternoon.

John glared at the sky. "No point in moving forward now."

"Damn." I threw my own glare skyward. "Pity we've lost a day."

He shrugged, and a faint smile brightened his expression. "Oh, I don't know if I'd say it was lost."

Our eyes met.

John quickly cleared his throat and dropped his gaze, gesturing emphatically at the repaired mech. "I mean, now if it breaks down like this again, in worse conditions, I know how to fix it."

"Right, right. Better here than knee-deep in snow."

"Precisely." His expression wavered slightly. "Anyhow, we should set up camp. While there's…" He gestured skyward. "While there's enough light."

Our eyes met again, but neither of us spoke. We set up, and while John chained the mech to a nearby tree, I put our bedrolls down inside the tent. Since we'd barely moved today, I wasn't nearly as exhausted as I had been. Still aching from the last two weeks, but better rested than I'd been since before John paid his way into my bed. The slowdown was frustrating, but the unexpected rest welcome.

Decidedly less dread than before twisted in my chest as I slid the white bottle under my bedroll, this time making sure it was well within reach. Without the exhaustion of a day's traveling, I couldn't help hoping he'd ask me to earn my wages.

When night fell and we bedded down, John lay beside me but didn't move to close the distance between us. Silence descended. Neither of us spoke. Neither of us moved. His breathing slowed, but it hadn't yet fallen into that rhythm of sleep I'd memorized over the last two weeks. He was still awake, still distant, still not laying a hand on me. Where previously relief would have settled in my chest, now there burned a mixture of confusion and disappointment.

Finally, I couldn't stand the silence or the sliver of warm space between us any longer. I took a breath. "John?"

"Hmm?"

I moistened my lips. "Why did you agree to hire me on?"

"You offered to work for half the wages of the other men. On my budget, I'd have been a fool not to hire you."

I couldn't argue with that. "But is that the only reason?"

John was quiet for a moment. Then the fur and bedroll rustled as he shifted, and when his shadow rose slightly beside me, I guessed he'd turned onto his side and propped himself up on his elbow. "Why do you ask?"

"I mean, given how we…met, I'm not certain if you expect me to…" I was thankful for the darkness—judging by the heat in my face, I must have been crimson.

"I didn't bring you along to be my whore," he whispered, a note of horror in his tone.

I exhaled, not sure how much of it was relief and how much was disappointment. "Oh."

"I suppose I should have made myself clear. I…never meant to lead you to believe I'd hired you on for any other reason than I'd have hired any of the men by the pier. That night in your bed was an indulgence I simply couldn't resist, even if my budget was painfully limited. I...just couldn't pass you by."

I curled my hands against my chest to still the trembling. "Would you be opposed?" I gulped. "If I offered?"

"I couldn't...I can't have you like a whore again. Not...not now."

I swallowed. "Why not?"

"Because after days in your company," he said softly, as if every word pained him, "I'm certain if I lay a hand on you, I'll want you. Not as a whore, just..." He took a breath. "If I touch you again, I'll want you as my own."

Heart pounding, I found John's hand in the darkness, and I guided it toward me. Neither of us made a sound, not even to draw or release a breath, and I closed my eyes as I pressed his warm fingertips to my cheek.

Unsteadily, John whispered, "Robert, we shouldn't."

"Says who?"

His fingers brushed my face, and he leaned closer, but hesitated. "This is..."

"I'm not offering to do it for pay." My voice shook as badly as his hand against my cheek. "I don't want to be your whore, John. I want to be your—"

He kissed me. For the first time ever, he kissed me, and for a long, long moment, we were still. Then he tilted his head slowly, and I parted my lips, and the kiss deepened until we both moaned and pulled each other closer. His hand slid into my hair, and as he rolled me onto my back, I wrapped my arms around him. He covered my body with his, and covered my lips with his hungry mouth. Shivers rippled up and down my spine as fingers tangled in hair and limbs tangled with each other.

With his weight over me, even beneath my bedroll, the ground was hard, but so were we. For two weeks, we'd kept our distance, and now we sought all the nearness we could get.

John bent to kiss my neck, and I gasped. Coarse chin, soft lips, warm breath, all on flesh I never knew could be so sensitive, and I moaned as he explored every inch from my jaw to my collar and back again.

"Oh, Robert," he breathed. "I've been dying to touch you again. You simply...you don't understand..." He trailed gentle kisses up the front of my throat to the underside of my jaw. "I've wanted you since the first time I laid eyes on you." His lips lingered against my chin. "And that didn't change after I'd had you. I want..." He shuddered, brushing his lips across mine. "I want to be inside you."

"Please..." I dug my fingers into his shoulders. Remembering the white bottle I'd again strategically placed within reach, I let go of one shoulder and fumbled around in the darkness until my fingertips found the cool glass.

John raised his head. "What are—" The bottle's top rattled, and John released a low growl. "You brought it. Thank *God*."

He pushed himself up off me. Frantically, desperately, we stripped out of our clothes, and when we came back together, hot flesh against hot flesh had never been so arousing. We kissed with an eagerness I'd never experienced. Giving as much as taking, wanting as much as needing. Our hands were shaking—his on my face, mine in his hair. Every time his hips moved, his hard cock rubbed against mine, and so I pressed my own hips to his, silently begging him to keep moving.

Then, arms around me, John rolled onto his back, and I was over him. Still beneath the fur blanket, we were on his bedroll now. He reached back toward my side, fumbling in the darkness, and a second later, the bottle's top clinked. I bit my lip as vague, shadowy movements in the darkness hinted at John pouring some of the liquid into his hand. My teeth chattered, but it had nothing to do with the chilly air around us. The blanket and John's body kept me warm while anticipation made my heart beat faster, and by the time he set the bottle aside, I was about to go mad.

His hand snaked over my thigh and cupped my buttock, and he nudged me forward. I rested my weight on my forearms and found his mouth with my own, and as I kissed him hard, his other hand slid between us. His fingertips drifted along my cock but didn't stop. The hand on my hip nudged me again, and I leaned further forward.

John's lips met the side of my throat in the same instant his slick, cool fingers found my entrance. I closed my eyes and sucked in a breath, and when his fingers pressed gently, I leaned against them, exhaling as one fingertip slid past the tight ring of muscle. Before I'd caught my breath, he added a second finger, and I arched against him as he kissed my neck and teased me with slow, slippery strokes.

Without any conscious thought, I moved my hips, desperate for more, more, more. His hand stilled, and he let me ride his fingers. His other hand closed around my cock, and the dual pleasure of being stroked and fingered turned the darkness to tear-blurred silver and white.

"Do you like that?" he whispered, breathing hard below me.

"God *yes.*" Stretched and slick and desperate for him, I wanted him inside me, but this...this felt so damned good. It felt so goddamned— "Fuck me, John." The words burst out of me, and the world echoed with the plea I'd never allowed myself to speak before. "Please, please, fuck me."

John withdrew his fingers. The bottle's top rattled, and we both shuddered as he lubricated his hard cock. Then with a hand on my hip, he guided me up, down again, and onto his cock.

I sat up straighter, the thick fur blanket sliding off my back and exposing my skin to the cold of the night. The bitter chill hardened my nipples and raised gooseflesh on my shoulders, but the rest of my body was warm against John's, and he was inside me, sliding deeper and filling me, and we could have been out in the falling snow for all I cared.

Taking him all the way inside me, I moaned softly.

"Am I hurting you?" he whispered. "Tell me if I…please—"

"No, you're not." I gasped for breath and rose again. "Not…oh, you feel perfect…" Throwing my head back, I came down on his cock. Again. Again. Again. "Oh God…"

He drew me down to kiss him, sliding a hand around the back of my neck and gripping my hip with the other.

"I don't know what you've done to me, Robert," he murmured into my kiss. "The moment I walked into that saloon, I wanted you." He thrust up. "And every day of this journey, I've been going mad wanting you again, and having you now…" He groaned, pulling my hips down on his cock as he thrust up. "Having you now, I just…oh God, I can barely stand it…"

Words eluded me, and it took all I had just to whimper with the pleasure of taking his cock again and again, of having him below me and against me and inside me. My throat constricted around my breath. My eyes watered, rolled back. I swore, and when John released a low growl from the back of his throat and forced himself deeper inside me, I shattered.

Trembling and moaning, I collapsed over him, and he kept moving, kept fucking me from below, until he gripped my hips painfully tight and pulled me against him. He panted in sharp, hot huffs, and his cock pulsed inside me.

I touched my forehead to his, and John wrapped his arms around me.

"This should…" He paused to catch his breath. "This should keep the nights warmer from here on out."

I just laughed and pulled him into another kiss.

Chapter 12

Daybreak came much too soon. Under any other circumstances, I'd have suggested we lie here for hours, wrapped up in each other beneath the blanket, but of course, we couldn't.

Outside, mechs were already clanging and sputtering past us. Men walked and grumbled. Horse hooves and dog paws crunched on snow. Before long, the trail would be crowded with men and machines. Comfortable as we were, we had to move on.

Besides, the longer we lingered this far south, the worse the weather would be when we reached the north, so we finally pulled away from each other and rose for the day. Thankfully, our clothes were still under the blanket when we awoke. Nothing would put an unpleasant end to a wonderful night like slipping into cold clothes.

Out of the corner of my eye, I watched John dress. He'd long ago abandoned the dignified silk and embroidery he'd worn when he'd stepped into my world. He dressed like any other man on the trail now—thicker trousers and a plain, unembellished shirt beneath a long coat not unlike my own.

We each had a set of brass goggles hanging around our necks by thick leather straps. Snow wasn't falling yet, but it could start with little warning, so we kept them at the ready in case we needed to fend off snow blindness.

Many of the men grew out beards in preparation for the bitter northern cold, but not John. He tried a few times. Day by day, the shadow on his jaw would darken until, after a few hours of cursing and scratching at it when it scuffed against his collar, he'd dig out a razor and shear it off.

He'd shaved it yesterday morning, and now had only a dusting of stubble around his lips and along his jaw. Even like this, unshaven and dressed like any other stampeder, he'd have stood out in any crowd. Fatigue and cold didn't stop him from carrying himself the very same way he had when he'd strolled into the saloon, as if to tell the world it would take more than a thousand-mile journey to hunch his back. Once in a while, he even pulled out that pocket watch, withdrawing it from the breast pocket of his jacket and casually glancing at it like a bored man at a dinner party.

This morning was no different, even if his gait was a little stiffer and slower than usual as we hit the trail. My own hips and back ached, but I wasn't about to complain.

The conversation that had carried us over miles and miles dwindled in the wake of the night we'd spent together. We exchanged looks across the mech, and those looks both promised and demanded more as soon as possible. I wondered a few times if we might throw caution and haste to the wind and spend the afternoon like we'd spent last night.

But we couldn't afford to lose more time, so for now, we walked.

John and I were lovers now, but for how long? Rich or poor, when this was all over, John would go back to Chicago and I'd...I'd find my own path. To somewhere.

I sighed, nestling my face into my high collar, hoping he thought I was hiding from the biting wind instead of covering up my frustration.

Even if I followed him back to Chicago, a professor struggling to stay in his university's good graces couldn't risk a lover like me. That assumed he'd even *want* me to come with him, and I didn't let myself hope he would. I could dream, but I knew as well as John surely did, that this would end when the trail did.

In silence, we continued north, but by noon, sheer boredom nudged us back into conversation just like our occasional pushes nudged the wandering mech back onto the trail. We talked of mundane topics, as we always had, but things had undeniably changed. That much was clear every time our eyes met over the mech and our conversation faded away.

But the future would be dealt with when it arrived. For now, I told myself, there were many miles and many days ahead, and for the duration, John and I had each other. Short of striking it filthy rich in Dawson City, there wasn't much more I could ask for.

Day by day, both the weather and terrain worsened. Hills were steeper and longer. Rain fell with more force. The wind bit at us until we pulled our goggles over our eyes and tucked our faces beneath our collars. The ground thawed, then froze, and slippery mud became treacherous frozen ground.

John and I spent every night wrapped tight in each other's arms. Sometimes for pleasure, always for warmth. Our bodies ached, and cold and exhaustion kept us from a lover's embrace more often than not. It was frequently tempting to fire up the heating device, so tempting, but we couldn't waste coal, so we shivered together beneath the fur blanket. In spite of the cold, I found a small, delicious thrill in his slow, soft breaths on my neck while he slept. There were less pleasant ways to spend a night.

Then the snow came. The mech creaked and groaned, protesting every slow step. It slipped and slid across the trail, making me dread the steep, dangerous crossing of the Chilkoot.

Mile after mile, the trail was more and more congested with men, animals, and mechs, just like it had been when we'd left Ketchikan. Roads and other trails converged with this one, which meant we were getting close to the pass.

Sure enough, early one afternoon, we rounded a bend and a crooked, hand-painted sign came into view: *Chilkoot Pass – 6 miles*

Not half a day, and we'd be at the foot of the pass. I shivered. The Chilkoot would be by far the most arduous part of our journey, though there was also the river and its rapids that would take us the very last stretch to Dawson City.

An expansive tent city sprawled across the snowy terrain just beyond the sign. Tents were erected in long, irregular rows. Rickety buildings had been put up around the perimeter of the camp, plus a few scattered amongst the tents, where outfitters, prostitutes, and makeshift saloon owners made a killing off hungry, thirsty, and frisky stampeders.

At the entrance to the tent city was a more solid structure, this one bearing the distinctive flag of the Canadian territories, with its red background, yellow coat of arms, and the Union Jack in one corner. This must be the place where we had to obtain approval to cross the pass. The North-West Mounted Police had originally set up their checkpoint on top of the pass, but then they'd moved it to a few miles south.

This technically put them on the wrong side of the hotly disputed Canadian-Alaskan border, but for safety and efficiency's sake, they were allowed to conduct their inspections here so they could carefully ration the number of teams allowed on the pass at a given time. Otherwise, too many mechs that never should have been allowed to ascend the mountain made it onto the pass. After someone's mech lost control and went crashing down the trail last year, killing dozens, the Mounties inspected every machine before it was allowed to climb the mountain, and they kept a strict limit of twenty mechs at a time on the Golden Staircase, the fifteen hundred steps carved into the ice from Chilkoot's base to its peak.

Every team of stampeders had to pass through this checkpoint and obtain authorization to cross the pass. The Mounties had no qualms about turning away sparsely provisioned teams, lame horses, and malfunctioning mechs. So the outfitters said, anyway.

But the mech inspections *were* mandatory, and so, like everyone else, John and I put our names on the inspection list and waited outside the encampment. If we passed, we'd be allowed to set up camp within the designated boundaries and wait for our turn to cross into Canada. If we failed, there was another camp where we could stay until we either repaired our mech or turned back.

John was confident we had everything we needed, and the repairs didn't concern him. Still, as we sat on the raised side of our mech, chewing on beef jerky and waiting our turn, he was unusually quiet. Tense, even. I couldn't decide if he was concerned about the inspection for some reason, or if he was just ready to set up camp and relax for the remainder of the day.

He wasn't alone in his silence. With the urgent need to get to the gold fields, not to mention the bitter cold and the frustration at being held up, most of the people waiting weren't interested in conversation. The mouthwatering scents of hot food and campfires taunting us from the other side of the fence didn't help. Over the echoing rumble of idling mechs came voices and the sounds of utensils tinkling against bowls; men engaged in rest and relaxation instead of grueling travels or the maddening tedium out here. Those among us who did speak complained about everything from the snow beneath our feet to the men conducting the inspections.

"They're strict, these ones," a grizzled man muttered a few paces away from me. "Just today, they've turned back three teams because of stripped bolts."

"Better to be turned back now," another man replied, "than break down in the Yukon."

The first sniffed sharply and shook his head. "They just want to keep us from the gold so the Canadians can get to it first."

John rolled his eyes but didn't say anything. He bit down on a piece of beef jerky and gnawed on it as he watched the Mounties inspect a team ahead of us.

Three uniformed men conducted the inspections. One of them inspected the mech, scrutinizing every gear and cog, examining the boiler and its lines, and testing legs and joints. Another Mountie went through the team's papers and documents while the third combed through the piles, bags, and crates of provisions, ticking items off a list in his hand. Whether they were looking for contraband or truly counting out a year's worth of supplies, I couldn't tell.

The third Mountie beckoned to the owner of the mech, and indicated a sealed crate tucked beneath a few bags of flour. John fidgeted beside me as the Mountie ordered the owner to open the box.

The man obeyed. He put the crate on the ground, then dug out a pry bar and used that to pop the nails and open the box. The contents, which were mostly tools for repairing the mech, were laid out for the Mountie—and the gathered crowd—to see. The inspector picked up one of three flasks and unscrewed the top. He sniffed it and flinched like it was stronger than he'd anticipated.

"How much alcohol do you have in your possession?" he asked as he screwed the cap back on.

"Just what's in there, sir," the owner said. "Three flasks. We're saving 'em to celebrate in Dawson."

The Mountie grunted and handed the flask back to him. "All right, then. Pack it up. One too many firearms, though. Going to have to leave one behind."

"Leave one behind?" The owner scoffed. "Are you mad?" He gestured sharply to the north. "There's *grizzlies* up there. And bandits!"

"There's also laws." The first Mountie eyed him coolly. "And our laws limit each man to three guns apiece."

The owner huffed and glared at each of the Mounties in turn. "Then what do you recommend I do with it? Throw it in the snow? Give it away?"

The one who'd announced the excess firearm nodded toward the encampment. "There are three outfitters who'd buy it from you outright. Plenty of men who might trade food or coal for it."

The other wrote something on the inspection sheet and handed it to the owner. "You'll be required a second inspection before you leave for the pass. See to it the gun isn't among your provisions and you have a receipt for its sale or trade, and you're permitted to enter Canada."

Snatching the sheet away, the owner gestured for his team to join him. They put everything back into the mech, fired it up, and walked beside it into the encampment.

Beside me, John fidgeted.

Keeping my voice low, I asked, "What's wrong?"

"I thought they only checked to make sure the mech is sound and our required provisions are accounted for." He drummed his fingers on the side of the mech. "No one said anything about checking for contraband."

I turned to him, eyebrows up. "Do...do we have contraband?"

"No, but not every item on our mech is one I want brandished for all to see."

His eyes darted toward the locked box between us.

"So what do we do?"

John shook his head. "I don't know."

The Mountie scowled as he watched the team go, then shook his head and picked up the list of names. "Fauth and Belton."

John blew out a breath and hoisted himself off the mech. "Here we go."

We stopped in front of the Mounties, and I set the brake. As the brass spider idled, we both stood back to let the inspectors do their job.

All the while, John chewed his thumbnail, deep crevices forming between his eyebrows.

"What's wrong?" I asked quietly.

He put up a hand and shook his head, but said nothing. The tautness of his lips did nothing to comfort me. Neither did his silence. Or the wary glances he kept throwing toward the gathered crowd.

One of the Mounties withdrew the locked wooden box from the mech. He dropped it unceremoniously in the snow, which brought an aggravated growl from the back of John's throat.

"You." The Mountie gestured sharply at John, then at the box. "Open that."

John stiffened. "Is that necessary?"

The Mountie raised an eyebrow. "It is now."

"Why?" John set his jaw. "I have the necessary provisions. I don't see why—"

"Excess provisions and contraband," the Mountie snapped. "We can't have people taking more than they can carry over the pass, and you've already reached your quota for weapons." He nodded toward the guns, which another Mountie inspected, and glared at John. "Open. The box."

"There's only scientific instruments in there," John said quietly. "They're quite delicate, and I—"

"Open the box, Mr.—" The Mountie glanced at the paper in his hand. "Open the box, *Dr.* Fauth."

John took a deep breath. "May I open it in there?" He indicated their inspection station with a sharp nod.

The Mountie's eyes narrowed. "Open it here, or consider it confiscated."

John swore again. Then, muttering a few curses, he pulled the key the pocket of his trousers. As he knelt beside the box, voices rippled through the crowd. Necks craned. Curious eyes peered.

The lock clicked, and hinges squeaked as he raised the box's lid.

"Take it out," the Mountie said tersely.

John exhaled. He lifted the device and cradled it on one arm as he carefully unwound its red shroud. Murmurs and whispers fluttered around us, and all eyes were on John.

Just before he lifted the last layer of fabric away, he cast one more wary glance at the gathered crowd. His lips thinned, and when his eyes met mine for a fleeting moment, the concern in his raised the hairs on the back of my neck. He took a deep breath, then pulled off the sheet of red and let it fall into the box.

Everyone stared at the device. The Mountie extended his hand.

John held the device to his chest, eyes darting left and right. "This is a delicate scientific instrument."

"And until it's inspected, it's contraband."

John clenched his jaw, but then he sighed and held out the device.

The Mountie took it and turned it in his hands, sunlight glinting off its brass casing and glass display. "What is it?"

John hesitated, absently tugging at his glove as if he needed to occupy his hands. Then his shoulders sank slightly, and he lowered his voice. "It detects noble metals in soil."

"Noble metals?" The Mountie eyed him. "Gold, then?"

Voices rippled around us with greater enthusiasm, and more heads turned.

"A gold detector?" somebody asked.

"A machine that finds gold?" someone else called out.

Shifting his weight, John spoke through gritted teeth. "Platinum, mostly. Rhodium, iridium, things of that nature."

The Mountie furrowed his brow and regarded the device curiously. "How does it work?"

John released a sharp, impatient breath. "It detects the metals based on their chemical nobility. How they react to a specific charge and the solution that's in the glass capsule at the top."

"Peculiar," the Mountie murmured.

"But will it find gold?" another voice shouted.

"It does no such thing," John barked. "It identifies traces of *platinum*."

The Mountie raised an eyebrow. "And what good will it do you in the Klondike?"

"Because platinum is found in gold deposits." More impatience seeped into John's voice. "Which is why I'm going there to look for it."

"So if it finds platinum," the other Mountie said, loud enough to make John cringe, "wouldn't that mean there's gold nearby?"

Shouts and murmurs rippled through the crowd. John closed his eyes, released a long breath through his nose. Then he glared at the first Mountie.

"May I have my device back?" he asked through his teeth. "It's very delicate. I didn't carry it all this way to have it break before I've even crossed the pass."

The Mountie's lip curled into a snarl, but when his gaze swept over the increasingly agitated crowd, he didn't argue. He thrust the device back into John's hands. "Everything is as it should be." He signed the bottom of the tattered form and handed it back to John. "Put up your tent where there's space. You'll be informed when your number is up to take the machine over the mountain."

"Thank you," John muttered. He looked at me and gave a sharp nod toward the camp. "Let's go."

With every voice whispering about the device in our mech, and every eye on our backs, we entered the encampment to wait our turn to go over the pass.

"Now what?" I asked.

John sighed. "Now we have to be extra vigilant. The men who threatened you back in Ketchikan?" He shook his head. "I suspect that as long as we're inside this encampment, they're the least of our worries."

Chapter 13

Most of the outfitters who'd set up shop in the encampment sold their wares for double or triple the going price in Seattle. Stampeders who'd run low on supplies had no choice but to pay such exorbitant prices, but even those of us who didn't need anything to gain access to Canada found something to spend money on—if not the whiskey and whores, then the shoes that hadn't been battered by hundreds of miles of rocks and mud.

For both John and me, our luxury of choice came in the form of steaming hot baths. A dark-eyed old woman rented out four immense tubs like Beatrice rented out the girls and me in Seattle, and men lined up around the building in the shin-deep snow to exchange a nickel for ten minutes.

Even standing in the line was worthwhile—after waiting outside in the bitter cold, one would eventually move into the building, where the line stood right against the rumbling twin boilers that kept the baths heated. They ran on wood instead of coal, and the old woman's daughters and son constantly stoked the fires to keep them roaring beneath the boilers. Heat radiated off the backs of the two huge machines, and if the proprietor wanted to, she could have charged men just to stand within the building.

Raggedy curtains had been draped from the ramshackle ceiling, hanging between each tub to offer some semblance of privacy. At the end of each curtain rod hung a bell, which the proprietor or one of her daughters rang when a patron's time was nearly up. One clang signaled he had one minute left, two clangs meant his time was up. Heaven help the man who tried to stay beyond his allotted time—the proprietor had a voice like a shotgun and a demeanor that removed any doubt from her threats to beat someone with the shovel beside the door.

After several men had gone through, the water would be emptied and refilled. Within ten minutes, the newly filled tub would be steaming and ready for the next patron. As luck would have it, on my first trip to the boiler house, one of the tubs had just been emptied and refilled with clean, hot water. I paid the proprietor, stripped off my clothes, and eased myself into the metal tub. It stung my cold-nipped skin, but I just sighed and lay back against the tub's edge.

The only way it could have been better was if I'd been sharing it with John. Oh, that would have been a dream. Resting against his body instead of the hard metal, his arms around me in the hot water, his breath cooling the perspiration on the side of my neck. I shivered at the thought.

Clang! The bell startled me out of the warmth of my mind. I sat up, reaching for the towel I'd brought with me, and—

Oh, Christ. Heat rushed into my cheeks that had nothing to do with the water around me. I took a deep breath, thinking of anything that could cool the effect John had on me, but the damage was done.

I closed my eyes, breathing deeply again. Not that I was the only man in this encampment who'd ever been aroused, but I was—rationally or not—afraid they'd know who had given me these insatiable thoughts. Men in this place were short-tempered from exhaustion, and half were looking for a fight. One of "our kind" among them was as good a reason as any, so—

Clang! Clang!

Fuck. Better to get out and risk someone seeing, than stay in and risk the woman shouting at me, drawing attention, and *everyone* seeing.

I stood and quickly pulled the towel around my waist, but not before I caught the eye of the woman's eldest daughter. Her lips pulled into a knowing smirk, and she batted her eyes at me. Face burning even hotter, I dropped my gaze and grabbed my clothes. There was a room off to the side where men could get dressed instead of staying beside a tub and keeping the next patron from his turn.

I dried off quickly and dressed, all the while cursing the bitter cold that would no doubt keep John and me from doing anything beyond keeping each other warm, though at least it would help me calm down below the belt. For now, anyway. Damn our limited supply of coal— that heating device would've been very, very useful tonight.

I laced up my boots and picked up my coat. As I started toward the door, a bear of a man stepped in front of me.

"I know you," he said.

My blood turned cold. The grizzled face was familiar, but I couldn't place him. Probably just someone I'd seen around the camp.

I swallowed hard. "I...beg your pardon?"

He gestured with his chin toward the other side of the encampment. "You're with that scientist, aren't you?"

I released my breath. Better to be recognized as John's traveling companion than someone who might be interested in selling a service.

"I am, yes." I pulled my jacket on.

The man grunted. His eyes narrowed, and I couldn't help drawing back. Maybe it would have been better if he'd tried to proposition me. Some thought deepened the creases between his thick, bushy eyebrows, and I didn't want to wait for that thought to come to fruition.

"If you'll excuse me." I put on my hat and started for the door, but he caught my arm.

"Hey, Turner," he called to someone else.

Another man appeared, blocking the doorway.

The one gripping my arm said, "He's that kid who was with that scientist. The one with the gold finder."

My blood flowed even colder.

The man called Turner looked at me. "We want that gold finder. We'll pay you three hundred dollars and half of whatever we find in Dawson City."

I swallowed. Three hundred dollars? Lord, how many men would I have to take into my bed to come up with an amount like that?

"Do we have a deal?" the other man asked.

"No." I gritted my teeth. "The device isn't for sale."

"I'm not asking if it's for sale." Turner's tone was menacing. "I'm asking you to get it for me, and I'll pay you for your trouble."

"You're asking me to steal it."

He nodded.

"No." I jerked my arm away from the other man. "The device isn't for sale, and I'm not stealing it from him."

He snatched my arm again, gripping it harder this time. "Maybe we're not making ourselves clear."

Turner narrowed his eyes. "Perhaps 'asking' isn't the word we should be using."

Fear crackled along the length of my spine. But then I remembered a piece of advice Gladys had given me when we were both between bedmates one night in the brothel.

"Let 'em know you're intimidated or scared," she'd said, "and they'll keep at you 'til you break down and give 'em what they want."

I took a breath and wrenched my arm away again. I stepped toward Turner so we were almost nose to nose. "The instrument is not for sale, nor is my loyalty to its owner. You want something that detects gold? Build it yourself."

I didn't wait for a response. I shoved past them, pulling my coat around me on my way outside. Shoulders bunched against the cold and chest tight with both fear and fury, I nestled my face into my collar and swore under my breath as I hurried toward John and the campsite. That encounter had ruined all the comfort I'd gained in the hot water, and the muscles in my neck and shoulders were taut as cables. On the bright side, at least it had taken care of my troublesome erection.

Not a moment too soon, I reached our campsite.

John sat beside the fire, one foot on the locked box and a tattered book in his hands. As I approached, he looked up, and it only took a heartbeat for concern to take over his expression.

"Something wrong?" he asked, a note of alarm in his voice.

I sat beside him, the box and rifle between us, and whispered, "We need to keep an eye on your instruments."

"I know," he grumbled. "Word is spreading like wildfire around the camp." Furrowing his brow, he held my gaze in the firelight. "What's wrong, though? You look shaken."

"Someone just tried to pay me to steal the device from you." I held my hands out over the fire to regain some warmth. "*Again.*"

His eyebrows shot up. "Are you all right? Did they—"

"I'm fine." I waved a hand. "They just...rattled me a bit, that's all."

John swore under his breath. "Damn Mounties. I could've shot the bastard for revealing the device to half the encampment."

"You might have warned me before that it was so fragile. If I'd known it was such a delicate instrument, I'd have been more careful with it."

John laughed. "Oh, it's not delicate at all. I didn't want that ogre manhandling it, but I knew there was no chance of it surviving this journey unless it was hardy enough to withstand whatever happened along the way." He looked around, as if someone might be waiting in the shadows to snatch it away. "Not much I can do if it winds up in another man's hands, though."

"True."

John met my eyes. "And the men who saw the device at the gate aren't the only ones we'll have to look out for."

"What do you mean?"

He held my gaze.

A piece fell into place, and icicles formed along my spine. "John..."

"I saw one of Sidney's men earlier."

I swallowed. "You're certain?"

"I thought I was imagining it, but then I saw him again." He chewed his lip. "They're keeping their distance for now. Probably because there are too many people around. But..."

"But they're here."

John nodded. Sighing, he ran a hand through his hair. "Damn it. I should have just gone into business manufacturing gold finders and selling them to stampeders instead of continuing with the university. I'd be a wealthy man, and I never would have had to leave the comfort of Seattle."

"But you wouldn't find the platinum you're looking for."

"No, perhaps not." He shrugged, then sighed again. "But maybe I'd have been able to afford to build a spare in case one was stolen."

"Or make enough money, you wouldn't need to do your research."

"Oh, it's not that simple." He gazed into the fire. "Were I a wealthy man who didn't need to work another day in his life, I'd still be tinkering in my lab." He laughed softly. "Just wouldn't have to spend so much time chasing down everything I need. I could have a whole staff of miners to hunt down the necessary platinum."

I watched the fire's reflection in his distant, unfocused eyes. "You'd keep working? Even if you didn't need to?"

He nodded. "I'm not the kind of man who can be idle, Robert. I need to do things." He held up his hands, gesturing like he were holding an object and tinkering with it. "I need to…make things. Discover things. Do you know what I mean?"

"I suppose I understand. I can't imagine there's anything less satisfying than being idle."

"No, nothing at all. I'd go mad." He paused. "What would you do? If you didn't have to work to survive?"

I shrugged. "I don't know, I think I'd be content if I could just spend some time looking at the things that are already around me. I don't need to make something new, I want to see what's already there." I gestured past the fire, as if that wave of my hand could indicate the universe beyond the encampment. "See the world." Turning to him, I added, "See the things other people have made."

He cocked his head, regarding me curiously. "What things? I mean, anything in particular?"

"Would everything be too easy?" I asked, chuckling.

John smiled. "Not at all. I've done a fair bit of traveling myself, and the more I see, the more I want to see."

"I envy you. I've been as far west as Seattle and as far north as, well, here. That's all."

"You have plenty of time. With any luck, we'll both be wealthy men soon, and then you'll have the world at your fingertips."

"One can only hope."

"Indeed." His smile faded and his gaze shifted toward the fire. "One can only hope."

Chapter 14

The nights were painfully cold now, even with John's body against mine beneath the thick furs—he'd bought a second from the encampment's outfitters—and with our clothes and coats on. More than once, I wanted to beg him to put on the heating device, but I knew as well as he did that we couldn't waste coal. We had enough money for baths and whiskey, but coal was scarce. Even the outfitters had none to sell, and already there were problems with theft amongst the other stampeders.

By far the biggest target for theft, though, was our tent. We didn't dare leave our provisions unattended because too many people knew about the device now. A steady stream of stampeders came by to offer John money, coal, land, daughters—anything imaginable for the gold finder. Whenever I was out of John's sight, people approached me with bribes, trying to persuade me to steal the finder in exchange for a cut of their resulting gold, not to mention similar prices to what they offered John. Offers became more desperate, and rejection was received with increasing hostility. More than one man's parting words held dangerous undercurrents, and by the end of the second day, rumors were rapidly circulating that John and I would be wise to watch our backs.

We both saw the three men who'd followed him from Chicago, but only fleeting glimpses. They may as well have been phantoms—slipping into shadows, disappearing into crowds. Maybe we were both going mad with paranoia. Maybe, maybe not.

Whatever the case, with all the potential thieves running around, it was no surprise when, on the second night, a half-dozen stampeders with whiskey on their breath and greed in their eyes descended on our campsite.

It happened in the blink of an eye. One minute, we were quietly reading beside our campfire, guns propped against our legs and the device hidden beneath a flour sack between us.

The next, we were surrounded.

I was certain we were dead men, but John held his ground. He stood and stepped in front of me, pistol drawn.

"Robert, stay there," he said tersely over his shoulder.

Though the encampment was a noisy, bustling place, the area around our tent was deathly silent.

One of the men stepped forward, rifle leveled at John. "Enough games. Give us the gold finder."

My heart thundered.

John planted his feet and stared down the barrel of the rifle. "I'm not giving you anything. Go back to your tents and—"

"Give us the gold finder," the man snarled from behind the rifle.

"It'd be useless in your hands." John didn't budge even when the man came closer. "It's not a magic gold finder. It is a scientific instrument."

"But it finds gold, doesn't it?" The menace in his voice gave me chills. A crowd gathered, the air alive with whispers and murmurs.

"It finds *platinum*," John said.

"And where there's platinum, there's gold, ain't there?" came the reply. "That's what you told the Mountie. A dozen men heard you."

"It won't find anything in a fool's hands," John said coolly. "Go ahead and shoot me. Then you'll have a worthless device."

The man balked. "You're lying. It's—"

"Hey! What's all this?" a voice broke in. Shifting only my eyes, afraid to move even my head, I turned to the left as a pair of Mounties shoved their way through the crowd. "What's going on here?"

"This." John waved a hand at the hostile crowd. "Now do you see why I didn't want your inspector revealing my damned device?"

The Mountie stiffened. He looked at the man holding the rifle. "Is that what this is about? That device?"

Color rushed into the man's cheeks.

Releasing a sharp breath, the Mountie approached the tense standoff. "Give me your weapons. Both of you."

John lowered his pistol and handed it, butt first, to the Mountie. The rifle stayed aimed at John's face.

"Give 'im the gun," the other Mountie ordered, and the creak of a hammer drawing back straightened every spine within earshot. When the man with the rifle saw the Mountie's weapon aimed at his head, he lowered his and then handed it over.

"Violence and disorder will not be tolerated," the first Mountie shouted to us and the gathered crowd. "Any man makes a threat to another's life or property, he'll be barred from Canada and this encampment, or he'll be shot where he stands."

No one said a word.

"That's what I thought." The Mountie turned to the men who'd threatened us. "Hand over your Chilkoot permits. You'll be transferred to the other camp tomorrow, and if you know what's good for you, you'll go south."

"What? We—"

"Enough." The Mountie glared at them. "Your permits. Now."

Everyone was still. I held my breath, certain another confrontation was about to erupt.

Then the leader of the team exhaled, and his shoulders slumped. "They're back at our campsite."

The Mountie ordered the other to follow them to their camp and revoke their permits. The team who'd invaded our campsite was summarily marched out of sight, and as the crowd dispersed, the Mountie turned to us. "For your safety, I think the two of you should move your camp." He nodded toward the inspection station. "I'll have a space cleared beside our station, and then my men will be close by in case there's a future problem."

"Thank you," John said. "But I think our best bet is to get away from this place and people who know about my device as quickly as possible."

The Mountie nodded. "We'll have you out of here and on the pass as soon as your names come up on—"

"Our names will come up at the same time as everyone who saw your men reveal my device," John said through gritted teeth. "You'd turn us out at the same time as them?"

"You're welcome to stay after they've gone. I can move you down the list."

"Down it, but not up it?"

"No." The Mountie shook his head and put up his gloved hands. "We aren't out to put men in danger, and we'll do what we can to prevent further problems, but I'll not risk a riot either."

John sighed. "Very well. We'll gather our things and move."

Before we started breaking down our campsite, John turned to me and put a hand on my shoulder. "You all right?"

"Me?" I stared at him. "I'm not the one who had a rifle pointed at me."

He shuddered, the first sign he'd given that the situation had frightened him like it would any other man. "Well. Hopefully that will be the end of it. Thank God for Mounties, eh?"

Thank God for Mounties, indeed. We settled into our new campsite beside the inspection station, and one of them strolled past every hour or so to make sure we were undisturbed. Whenever John or I left to visit the baths or an outfitter, an armed Mountie accompanied us.

None of this gave me an ounce of comfort. While no one dared bother us here, within the fence and with Mounties watching our every move, we couldn't stay here forever. Once we left, there would be no one to walk past and ward off trouble with a menacing stare or a hand on a gun. The three who pursued us wouldn't need to hide, and those who sought to steal the device had nothing to fear but whatever defenses two men could muster.

It was a strange world, I mused as light from our campfire flickered along the wall of the inspection station. I'd always known greed was a powerful thing, but out here, civilized men turned lawless in their frenzied hunger for the gold that was, we all hoped, not far beyond this pass.

And John, he was either a man with an admirable drive, or he was a complete fool. Or insane. Perhaps he was a bit of all three. He was willing to fight—fists, bullets, probably a grizzly if it came down to it—to keep safe the instrument that held his last chance to continue his work. The work that meant as much to him as the breath in his lungs and the blood in his veins. I shuddered at the thought of how the other night's confrontation might have ended had the Mounties not intervened. Not with John surrendering his device, that much I knew.

"You're quiet tonight." His voice startled me.

I turned, watching the campfire flicker across his face. "I'm curious about something."

He lowered his chin a little. "All right."

"I've now seen firsthand what Sidney's men and, well, other men will do to get your device."

John nodded.

I slowly drew my tongue along the inside of my lip. "What lengths will *you* go to?"

"What do you mean?"

"I mean, how far will you go to protect that thing?"

He held my gaze for a long moment. "This is my life's work, Robert. I didn't come all this way to fail."

"But at what cost?"

His eyes trailed from the fire to the flour sacks covering the box between us. Then they flicked up and met mine. "I suppose I'm willing to sacrifice as much as any man who makes this journey."

"I don't imagine many other men in this camp would take a bullet for anything they're carrying with them."

He laughed dryly. "I suppose it depends on what they're carrying with them."

"Are you suggesting you would take a bullet for that thing?"

He didn't answer right away. He faced the fire, but his gaze was distant.

"John." I resisted the urge to put a hand on his knee. "You wouldn't really. Would you?"

"It sounds foolish, I know. It sounds as foolish to my ears as it does to yours. But then I consider what's left if I lose my work. If I fail in Dawson City, then I'll lose my funding. If I lose my funding…"

"There are other universities, aren't there?"

"There are." He took a long swallow of whiskey from a flask. "But my reputation is widely known from one to the next." With an expression made of equal parts melancholy and fierce determination, he stared at the locked box between us. "This equipment is the only chance I have of finding the metal I need, and God only knows if the Klondike has any, let alone enough for my work." He turned toward the campfire again. Raising the flask to his lips, he added softly, "And it's only half a prayer's chance, but I have no choice. If the door closes in Chicago, it'll take a miracle for another to open elsewhere."

Every man had a fever that drove him to make this journey. It shouldn't have surprised me that John was no exception.

~*~

One of us went by the inspection station every hour to check for updates to the list of mechs authorized to leave for the pass, and finally, shortly before sundown on the fifth day, a Monday, our names appeared on the list for departure on Wednesday.

As I stepped out of the tent after tucking away the coal, John put a hand on my arm. "Keep this with you, especially after we leave." His voice was low in spite of the relative privacy of our protected campsite, and he slipped a pistol into my jacket pocket.

"I already have one. I—"

"I know." The firelight cast eerie shadows across his deathly serious expression. "But you'll be safer if you carry extra. I have the rifle and my own pistol." He exhaled. "I don't expect much trouble on the pass. Any man would be a fool to attack another on that mountain. But once we're past it, we won't have the Mounties looking over everyone's shoulders." He gestured with his chin toward the inspection station. "They're all that's stood between the thieves and us, and once we're out in the open, I don't want to take any chances."

"I'm staying with you, though."

John studied me. "We'll have to be extra vigilant. I'd rather run from ghosts than ignore real danger." He met my eyes in the low light. "If you decide you want to fall back or go ahead, put some distance between us until we reach the next town, I won't hold it against you."

"You can't handle the mech on your own. Especially not on the pass."

"I'll do what I can, but I can't put you in harm's way, Robert. I simply can't."

I put a gloved hand over his sleeve. "You hired me to help you get the mech to Dawson City. That, and it's carrying my provisions too. If someone tries to steal your instruments, your chances are better with two of us than facing them on your own."

"Yes, perhaps they are." He shook his head. "But if anyone's blood is going to be shed over this thing, it should be mine, not yours."

"Be that as it may, we're safer together," I said. "You can't control the mech and defend against thieves on your own, and if I go on alone, then I'm ripe for the picking by any bandit or grizzly."

John chewed his lip. I thought he might argue, but then he just blew out a breath and nodded. "All right. But keep both guns with you at all times, and—"

"John." I squeezed his arm. "I know. I'll be fine."

His lips thinned, and his brow creased with worry, but he didn't press the issue any further. Instead, he gestured toward the heart of the encampment, where men drank and baths steamed. "Why don't you go get a drink or enjoy some warmth? Get your fill while we still can."

"You probably need it more than I do. You go first."

He didn't argue. The tension in his neck and shoulders was visible from here, the cords standing out like bands of steel, and the hot water would do him good.

I could wait a little longer.

Chapter 15

From the Diary of Dr. Jonathon W. Fauth — October 14, 1898

Just as I suspected, word of the device has spread, and Robert and I have become the targets of everything from gossip to robbery attempts. For his own safety, I've urged him to again reconsider traveling with me, but he refuses.

At least for the time being, the device remains securely in my possession, though, locked away in our tent. Robert is well armed, and the Mounties are within earshot at all times, so I can leave for short periods without worrying unnecessarily.

In spite of the need for constant vigilance, we're both well aware of the need to rest while we still can. Monotony taxes us just as it does any man, and like everyone in the encampment, we've found ways to stave off boredom. Boredom and cold, both of which are in great abundance.

The luxurious hot baths I have indulged in the last few nights have been a wonderful opportunity to think. Standing in line, lying in the hot water, walking back; my body's idleness has been most productive for my mind. Just this evening, while up to my neck in steaming water, I thought of a new and perhaps more efficient design for the BT4 semiconductor, the one that's been troubling me the last half year. If it works as well as I suspect it will, it may eliminate the problems I've been encountering with the D192 device.

But...I'll get to that in a moment. Perhaps this isn't the place for me to write about this, but if I don't get these other thoughts off my mind now, I will surely go mad.

This man I've journeyed with, he's absolutely bewitched me. No, he's gone beyond bewitching. I cannot put into words what he's done to me. His gentle quietude is intoxicating, and I find myself loath to leave the campsite, not merely because I hesitate to let him out of my sight with the potential danger, but because I don't wish to let him out of my sight at all.

Never have I had a lover with whom I was content to simply lie in bed at night. Yet at the same time, I go mad when I *can't* touch him except through clothing. I must have spent half of last night cursing the frigid air that forced us to huddle together only for warmth, and all the while, the very scent and warmth of his body against mine was its own ecstasy.

He's driving me mad, I tell you. Oh, I could babble on for pages about how Robert can ask a question—perhaps about the university or Chicago, both of which pique his curiosity—and the mere sound of his voice renders me mute. Just the other night, he asked me about my past lovers, and wouldn't you know? I couldn't even remember their names. None of them! It took an embarrassing amount of stammering and racking my brain before I remembered Seamus's name. How absurd! He must have thought I was a loon, unable to remember the name of the last real lover I'd had.

I should be thinking of nothing but my goal. Platinum, semiconductors, telescreen communication. But I'm not, am I? No, I lie awake at night thinking of Robert and holding Robert. By day, I think of him, talk with him, simply exist in the same world as him. Oh, of course, I do think about my work—it drives me on even when this journey exhausts me—but my thoughts are not as focused as they ought to be.

But what is there to be done about it? I cannot simply pretend he isn't here. I cannot stop myself from wanting him like this, and I certainly cannot—

Look at me. What a schoolboy he's made me. Reduced to a babbling fool when I'd had every intention of documenting my earlier thought about the BT4 semiconductor. But there is no time now. Robert is on his way back, so I will finish my thoughts later. For now, I have but one night to spend with him before we are once again underway, and before our journey becomes truly dangerous.

One last night, and I dare not waste it.

Chapter 16

On my way back to the campsite with my Mountie escort on my heels, the bath's heat lingered beneath my skin like slowly cooling campfire embers. The cold tried to creep up my sleeves and under my collar, but I kept my hands fisted in my pockets and my face nestled into my jacket. Eyes down, face hidden, I avoided the cold as well as predatory looks from anyone who knew I was one of the men traveling with the gold detector. They didn't dare approach me now, not when the Mounties threatened to shoot or deport anyone who tried, but they still eyed John and me and whispered behind their hands.

More than ever, I didn't relish leaving the encampment.

At the campsite, my escort continued to the inspection station while I joined John by the tent. It was no surprise to see him beside the fire with his journal on his knee and the rifle leaning against his leg.

Then he turned to me, and a sly grin spread across his lips.

I furrowed my brow. "What?"

"Hmm?" His eyebrows jumped. Then he cleared his throat and shifted the book on his lap. "Nothing. Why?"

"You looked like you had something on your mind."

John laughed softly. "I'm a scientist, Robert. I always have something on my mind."

"Yes, but from the look in your eyes, I suspect you weren't thinking about anything scientific."

"What was I thinking, then?"

"You tell me."

He just smiled and returned his gaze to his journal.

I watched him, wondering what hid in that curious mind of his. Then I shook my head and continued past him to put my things beside my bedroll.

When I pushed back the flap and ducked into the tent, I fully expected the air within to be as bitterly cold as it was outside. To my surprise, a rush of gentle warmth, not unlike that which I'd enjoyed beside the fire, met my face.

Behind me, water splashed, then hissed, and the light of the campfire vanished, but the tent wasn't completely dark. Off to my right, the heating device's coils glowed orange, casting a faint amber blush over the bedrolls and provisions.

John stepped in behind me, and after he'd closed the tent flap, he slid his hands over my shoulders. "As cold as it is tonight, I thought we could spare a few pieces of coal for a little warmth." His lips brushed the side of my neck. "And perhaps have one night without so much"—his fingers drifted down my sleeves—"between us."

I bit my lip, tilting my head so his lips could explore more of the flesh above my collar.

"I know we should sleep," he murmured. "Tomorrow will be like no day we've endured thus far. But I..." He kissed my neck and wrapped his arms around me, pulling me against his chest.

Closing my eyes, I released a long breath as his lips traveled up and down the side of my neck. I didn't know if I wanted to get his attention, if I intended to say anything, or if I just needed to taste his name while he kissed my neck, but I put my hands over his and whispered, "John…"

"Before we cross the pass, I just…I need one more night with you."

I turned around in his arms, and our eyes met in the low light from the heating device. For a handful of heartbeats, neither of us spoke or even breathed.

Then John put his hand on my cheek and leaned in to kiss me.

We sank as one onto the fur blankets that lay across our bedrolls. I pushed his jacket over his shoulders, and as he shrugged it off, I started on the buttons of his shirt. Though the air beyond our tent was dangerously cold, we shed clothing without a care in the world, baring flesh to warmth that existed only for us.

John kissed me and laid me back on the fur. "I knew there was something about you the night we met," he whispered, dipping his head to kiss my neck again, "but I never imagined this."

"Neither did I." My breath caught as his chin—freshly shaved, but still deliciously coarse—grazed my throat. "I thought you were just another…well, just another john."

A breath of laughter warmed my neck. "That night, perhaps I was. But…" He pushed himself up and rested his weight on his forearm, his expression turning serious in the soft orange glow. With his other hand, he caressed my face. "Whatever happens after we leave here tomorrow, I couldn't live with myself if I didn't take advantage of every hour we have left tonight."

He didn't give me a chance to respond, instead sinking into a slow, passionate kiss. His tongue parted my lips, and gooseflesh rose on my neck and arms as I held him closer.

I'd never before had the chance to memorize a man's kiss—the way he tasted, the way his lips and tongue moved, those soft little sounds of pleasure—like I'd memorized John's. He could have found me on a dark street, caught me by surprise, and kissed me, and I'd have instantly known it was him. It didn't matter if his chin was thick with stubble or freshly shaved, or if his mouth tasted of whiskey like it sometimes did—I'd know John's kiss anywhere. The tip of his tongue teased mine like he knew it would make me shiver, and he too shivered sometimes, moaning against my lips or pulling in sharp breaths through his nose. I knew his scent, his taste, his voice, his touch. Like no other man before him, I knew *him*.

He broke the kiss. Our foreheads touched, and we panted against each other's lips. I couldn't say who trembled more. When I slid my hand into his hair and drew him back down to me, he kissed me, and we held each other tight as his kiss carried me away like no man's kiss had ever aspired to do.

Arousal became feverish, desperate need. I had to have him. Now. Deep inside me, breathing hard against my neck and fucking me into delirium. *Now.*

I nudged his shoulder, urging him to roll onto his back, but he didn't move.

"No." He clasped my hand in his and pinned it to the fur. "Tonight is about your pleasure."

I stared with wide eyes at the top of the tent. My pleasure?

John trailed soft kisses along my jaw. "Answer me truthfully, Robert," he whispered, pausing to drag his lip just below my ear. "Did you have lovers before you became a prostitute?"

My face burned, and I hoped that if he looked, the heating device would cast only the most discreet glow over my undoubtedly red cheeks. "I...no, I didn't."

"Never?"

I swallowed. "Never."

"A pity." He nibbled my earlobe, and I pulled in a breath as his hard cock pressed against mine. "That means no man has spent time giving you the pleasure you've given him." Hot breath rushed across the side of my neck.

"Fools, all of them, but no matter." He kissed where his breath had warmed, then lower, and still a little lower. When he reached my collarbone, he whispered, "Simply means the pleasure will be mine and mine alone."

"Oh, it's not—" I gasped as he gently pressed his teeth into my nipple. "The pleasure isn't *all* yours."

"I certainly hope not," he murmured. "That would defeat the entire purpose, now wouldn't it?"

I tried to speak, but he took my nipple between his teeth, and any words I might have found stopped in my throat. He teased me with his tongue, my head swirling with the combined softness of his tongue and the *just* slightly painful bite.

He continued moving down. "Is it safe to assume, then—" He kissed just above my navel. "—that no man has ever tasted you?"

I squirmed beneath him. "No one."

"Mmm." He kissed my skin again, then met my eyes in the dim light. "What a pity for them."

I pushed myself up on my elbows and stared down at him, lips parted in disbelief as he inched lower, lower, lower.

He planted a soft kiss just beside the base of my cock. Eyes flicking up to meet mine, he pressed his lips to my hard shaft, and my stomach muscles contracted from just that light touch. Then he traced the length of my cock with his tongue, forcing every last breath out of my lungs. I wasn't used to being the one to lie back and be pleasured, to the idea of someone enjoying my arousal this way, and John's gentle, hungry enthusiasm drove me mad.

And he was only getting started. The things he did with his mouth were nothing short of breathtaking, and tears stung my eyes as John explored my cock, my testicles, the sensitive skin along my inner thighs. He fluttered his tongue here, circled with it there, kissed, sucked, *breathed.* He lapped at my testicles, flicking his tongue across skin that had never known such a sensation could exist.

He left no flesh unkissed, no skin unwarmed by soft breaths. I rested my hand in his hair and let my head fall back. I'd never imagined such a touch could be so…intense. And just when I didn't think I could stand another moment of it, he steadied my cock with one hand and took me slowly—oh God, so *slowly*—into his mouth, swallowing me almost to the hilt before rising off me and doing it again. The second time, he paused with only his lips around the head and teased me with his tongue, waiting until I whimpered softly before he continued his slow down-up-down motions.

He stopped, and when he sucked his own finger into his mouth, my breath caught. Then he teased my entrance with that moistened finger, and I whimpered as he took my cock in his mouth again at the same moment his finger pressed into me.

I'd always wondered why men loved this so much, why they asked, begged, commanded me to do it. I understood now. I couldn't imagine I'd ever done as much for a man as John did for me, though. He was…His mouth was…He…

"Oh God…" Screwing my eyes shut, I dug my teeth into my lower lip and grabbed handfuls of the fur beside me. We were far from anyone who might hear the soft moans and rustling of bodies moving together, but if I cried out like John's lips and tongue dared me to, a dozen men would come running. And God, oh God, nothing at all was the matter except that I was on the verge of losing every fragment of sanity I possessed.

He closed his hand around me and stroked rapidly, his palm sliding easily up and down the slick shaft as his fingers slipped in and out of me and his lips and tongue teased the most breathtaking sensations from the head of my cock. I collapsed onto the fur blanket, squeezing hot tears from my eyes as my back arched and my toes curled. My testicles tightened, my cock ached, and my entire body tensed. I craved release so badly I couldn't even breathe, and I couldn't beg him not to stop, and I couldn't tell him I was on the verge of falling to pieces, and I couldn't stop my climax if I wanted to, and I didn't want to, and I didn't stop it, and—

I clapped a hand over my mouth an instant before I would have let go of a cry. My body shook and shuddered, and John groaned softly as I spent on his tongue.

As soon as he sat up over me, I grabbed the back of his neck with both hands and dragged him down to me. His tongue was salty-sweet from my release, and he breathed as rapidly and unevenly as I did. Sliding his arms under my back, he pressed his cock against me and groaned into my kiss.

The heating device's warmth was tepid compared to the fiery heat of John's body against mine. I had never been so damned overwhelmed by...anything. Anyone.

"Fuck me." I clung to the back of his neck with trembling hands. "Please."

John released a low growl and claimed a deep, needy kiss. Twice, he tried to pull away, his breath catching like he was about to speak, and each time, he came back down for more. Finally, the third time, he kept himself away and, breathing hard, whispered, "Stay just like that. Don't...don't move."

I didn't move. He pulled the white bottle from beside the bedrolls where he must have stashed it. The bottle top scraped, the uneven sound revealing the unsteadiness of his hands.

The top clinked, and John moved over me. He sat up, and I rested one leg against each of his hips. His hand drifted up my inner thigh, and I closed my eyes, anticipating that first slippery, cool contact, and when it came, my back lifted off the fur. He didn't even let me catch my breath before he pushed one finger in. I moaned, squirming against him and trying to draw his finger in deeper. He withdrew it, then added another, and teased me *relentlessly*. In the wake of a climax, every motion of his fingers made me squirm and gasp.

The next groan was his, and he withdrew his fingers. "I can't wait another second." He barely breathed as he guided himself to me. "You can't even imagine, Robert, if I—*oh* God…" The head of his cock slid into me, and I couldn't say who trembled more or whose moan was more helpless. He pulled back a little, then slid in deeper, and we both released ragged breaths as he slowly buried himself to the hilt. One stroke, two, then a third, and with a shiver, he came down to me, seeking my mouth with his own. I wrapped my arms around him, and as we kissed, our bodies moved together, skin brushing skin and his cock sliding easily in and out of me.

Even as he fucked me and we touched every way two men could touch, it wasn't enough. Not nearly enough. Never enough. I raked my fingers through his hair, clawed at his back, dragged my hands down his arms. I wanted more of him. I needed to taste him and breathe him and feel every sharp, hot exhalation across my skin.

Then John groaned and shuddered, and I thought he was on the verge of climaxing, but instead, with a throaty growl, he grabbed my wrists and pinned them to the fur. His head fell beside mine, and his breath alternately warmed and cooled my neck as he thrust into me like a man possessed. I hooked my ankles behind his back, and he drove deeper, drove harder.

"Oh God, Robert," he breathed, nearly sobbing against my collarbone. "Oh God…"

I rocked my hips back, and he shuddered again. Deeper, harder, oh God, he fucked me mercilessly, until intense bordered on painful, until I'd have climaxed right then if I hadn't already, until he finally buried his face against my neck and muffled a helpless groan. His back arched above us, his hips trembling as he tried to force his pulsing cock just a little farther inside me.

Then he collapsed. I freed my wrists and wrapped my arms around him, and for the longest time, we just held on to each other. Panting, shaking, sweating, we held each other.

His lips found mine, and between light, breathless kisses, he murmured, "You're no one's whore, Robert."

"Not anymore."

"Not anymore." He stroked my hair with a trembling hand. "Now you're just...mine."

But for how long?

I banished the thought and kissed him again.

Eventually, John got up, and we cleaned ourselves off with a couple of rags he'd left near our bedrolls. Then we pulled the furs up over us and faced each other. His cheeks were still flushed—I had no doubt mine were too—and as warm as it was in here, inside our tent and beneath the blankets, it was hard to believe we were sleeping on frozen ground. Tomorrow, we'd trudge up the mountain, through the snow and ice, and by the time we set up camp for the night, we'd probably be numb from head to toe.

But here, tonight, we were warm and cozy.

John trailed his fingers down my cheek, and as he met my eyes, he smiled. I returned the smile, but a sinking feeling in my chest made me shift my gaze away.

"What's wrong?" he asked.

I swallowed and made myself look at him as I trailed my fingertips over his smooth jaw. "This is well and good tonight, but what happens when this is all over?"

Running his fingers through my hair, he shook his head. "I don't know."

We both knew how something like this would fare against reality. The deck was just too well stacked against us.

But I couldn't let that knowledge ruin our evening. If this was the last night we ever spent like this, naked and warm in each other's arms, then there was no sense wasting it on melancholy thoughts.

"I suppose," I said, pausing to moisten my lips, "we shouldn't think much further ahead than Dawson City. God only knows what will happen between here and there."

He laughed softly and bent to kiss me. "In that case, I look forward to sorting this dilemma in Dawson City, because I fully intend to get there with you beside me."

I grinned into his kiss. "All the more motivation for us both to make it in one piece."

With another quiet laugh, he said, "Indeed it is." He silenced any further conversation with a long kiss.

I tried not to let myself get too lost in fantasies about what might happen when all this was over. We had too many miles to go and too many dangers to face before we had any business trying to imagine the future, together or apart. And for that matter, John had come this far and faced all these dangers for his work—this was a man married to his work, and he'd all but said himself he'd chosen that work over lovers.

Once we'd finished in Dawson City, he'd go back to Chicago. Back to his laboratory. Back to the people who couldn't know about his "immoral conduct." There was no room for me in that world.

But that didn't stop me from hoping.

Chapter 17

The morning light found us tangled up in each other beneath the thick fur. Though we couldn't afford to waste time, neither of us could resist just one more kiss. That kiss became a touch, the touch became an embrace, and the embrace led to the first of many deep, breathtaking strokes of his cock.

Daylight illuminated everything the shadows had hidden last night, and this time, when he wasn't kissing me, he gazed down at me, and he didn't look away, not until a shudder forced his eyes closed the instant he spent inside me. And still we held on, long after we'd both caught our breath and the feverish need had cooled.

I'd never coupled with a man so tenderly, and yet so hungrily. Gentle and desperate, all at once, until he left me aching from exertion and yet aching for more.

But we had our permit to cross the pass, so we couldn't stay wrapped up together like this for long. After a few gentle kisses, and a few touches that *almost* kept us here, we made ourselves get up and dressed. John turned off the heating device, and we stepped out into the biting wind.

"My God." I hugged myself against the cold. "When this is all over, I'm going to go live someplace warm."

John laughed through chattering teeth. "I might not be far behind you. Let's break camp and get moving—the more we move, the warmer we'll be."

He was right, but only to a point. Standing still was miserably cold, moving only slightly less so, but I'd take any warmth I could get. We quickly took down our campsite, loaded up our mech, and made our way to the gate.

Several Mounties were stationed at the camp's edge. While I waited for one of them to go over our permits and paperwork, John pulled another aside. They stepped around beside the inspection shack, almost out of sight but not completely.

I watched from the corner of my eye as John leaned in close to him, whispering something in his ear, and their bodies *almost* shielded a quick transfer of something from John's hand to the Mountie's. Then they shook hands, exchanged a few words, and separated.

As John came back toward me, I raised my eyebrows, glancing at the Mountie. His back was turned, and I wondered if anyone else saw him slip what looked like a wad of bills into the pocket of his trousers.

But I didn't say anything until we'd passed through the gate. "What was that about? With the Mountie?"

"Never mind." John glanced at me and winked.

I planted my feet. "John, are—"

"I'll explain once we've gained some ground," he said quietly. "Keep going."

I hesitated. So far, though, John hadn't deceived me, and at least we were getting away from that damned camp, so I continued beside him and the mech.

After we'd gone half a mile or so, I turned to him. "All right. What was that exchange?"

John grinned at me over the mech. "I merely paid him to move our 'friends' down the list." He glanced over his shoulder as if someone might be around to hear him. "Assuming his word is good, I've bought us a head start."

"You're...you're serious."

He nodded, and a grin played at his lips. "Normally I wouldn't try to bribe a man of the law, but given the chaos that ensued thanks to their inspection..." He shrugged.

"I thought they were worried about riots."

"For letting us go before the hundred or so men ahead of us, yes. But keeping Sidney's men back?" He winked.

I chuckled. "Good work."

~*~

The brutal cold worsened as we neared the pass. The terrain was steeper, rockier, and icier, and our mech slipped and slid, as did those around us. By the time we reached the tiny settlement at the base of the Golden Staircase, the snow was high and I was exhausted.

At the base of the pass, an outfitter had set up a small shack and sold what reminded me of a logger's climbing spikes, but instead of a single long spike in front, they had many shorter ones beneath the sole.

"Interesting." John turned one of the boots over and over in his hands. He tried to flex the stiff sole. Touched the spikes with his gloved—and then bare—fingertips. Wiggled the spikes. Tugged at the straps.

The outfitter sighed impatiently. "I got people waiting, sir. You gonna buy 'em or not?"

John handed back the boot. "Four pair, please." Before I could ask why we needed so many, he turned to me. "Find the saw, if you would."

"The—" I blinked. "Uh, all right." While he and the outfitter handled the exchange, I went back to the mech and dug through a pack until I found the small hand saw. "What's this for?"

"Giving our mech some traction." He handed the money to the outfitter. "We'll each wear a pair, and we'll cut the others in half for the mech to wear."

The outfitter blinked. "Pardon?"

John grinned. "You've never thought to put them on a mech?"

"I…no, I can't say I have. Does it work?"

"Don't know yet." John handed me all but one of the pairs he'd just bought. "We'll find out in a moment. Put a pair on your feet, and cut the others in half. I'll secure them to the mech."

Though the mech's eight legs made it somewhat clumsy, it did offer a slight advantage for this task—John could easily pick up one leg to lash on the cleats, much like a farrier picking up a horse's hoof to put on a shoe.

Once the machine had been shod, John switched on the engine and tested it, letting it walk across the frozen ground. It moved slower than usual, having to work harder to pick up each foot, but it didn't slide, even when it hit a patch of ice.

"You really think this will work on the slope?" I asked.

"I think it'll work better than taking it up there barefoot." He glanced at the Golden Staircase and the men and mechs slowly making their way over the pass.

The outfitter shook his head. "Can't believe I never thought of that."

John chuckled and clapped the man's arm. "Well, if we don't come tumbling back down, assume it worked and sell the same to the men who come after us."

Shortly after we'd fitted our mech's feet with the spikes and lashed a pair to our own boots, it was our turn to head up the pass. Teams were sent onto the staircase a few at a time to ensure space between them and, I guessed, to keep damage and injury to a minimum if something happened. With clumsy, heavily-laden brass spiders creeping up the ice, that seemed wise to me. There wasn't much room for error—the stairs were narrow, having been carved before the mechs had become commonplace on the trail. The snow on either side was nearly to my chest, and any time the mech wobbled even slightly, it scraped the packed snow.

John walked in front of the mech, facing it and steadying it when it tried to wander, while I brought up the rear. As we started up the steps, my heart thundered, and it wasn't only because of the ice and the mech. Surely even the most desperate thieves wouldn't be foolish enough to try to attack us up here unless they wanted to be crushed by a mech for their trouble, but after the last few days, paranoia had become as natural as breathing.

"Doing all right back there?" John called out.

"Going slow, but doing fine. You?"

"Good here too. Slow and easy's the way to do it—I want us both over this pass in one piece, not over it first."

As it turned out, it was slow and easy or not at all. Every step up the Golden Staircase was more difficult than the last. We'd barely left the base camp before we were both out of breath. I was bundled against the cold, but couldn't avoid breathing in the frigid air, and my lungs ached as I worked my way up the ice stairs.

The mech was a blessing in disguise. Though it kept a fairly brisk pace on level ground, we'd been advised to put it in a lower gear for the climb. Since it was crawling up the stairs at a snail's pace, I had no choice but to go slow myself—much to the relief of my burning legs. For that matter, the team ahead of us had sleds instead of a mech; they moved even slower than we did, struggling to pull their heavy gear up the steps.

John's idea of putting spikes on the mech's feet proved to be brilliant. All along the staircase, men shouted and scrambled as they tried to keep their mechs from slipping and sliding. More than once, the entire caravan ground to a halt while a couple of teams untangled their mechs after one slid into another.

Ours, though, stayed sure and true. Its steps were slower, since the engine and gears had to work to pull the spikes out of the ice, but it didn't slide.

Step after step, we trudged upward.

Ahead of us, someone shouted.

I looked up just in time to see one of the sleds break loose. "John! Look out!"

He turned, and I thought I heard him curse as the sled and its pile of packs barreled straight toward him. Instead of trying to get out of the way, though, he crouched down, shoulder out like he was ready to catch a charging horse in the chest.

I threw the switch for the brake and vaulted onto the mech to try to pull John out of the way before the sled hit him. I wasn't quite fast enough, though—the sled collided with John and nearly knocked him off his feet. He grunted, digging his spikes into the steps and pushing back against the sled.

I stepped over our provisions and dropped down beside him in the narrow space between the walls of snow. I leaned into the sled, taking some of the weight off him, and he released a breath.

"You all right?"

"Yeah." He looked over his shoulder. "The mech. Is it—"

"Brake's on. It's not going anywhere."

"Good." He exhaled again. "Good work."

Above us, hurried footsteps came down the slope and skidded to a halt. "You all right down there?"

"Just get this damned thing off me," John threw back.

The weight on our shoulders lightened. With some more grunting and tugging from above, the sled moved back.

John dropped onto the step, rubbing his shoulder and grimacing.

I knelt beside him. "How bad is it?"

"I'll be…I'll be fine." He closed his eyes and released a long breath. "Doesn't feel like anything's broken."

"Thank God for—"

"Are you boys all right?" A bearded prospector appeared on the step above us. "We're terribly sorry. Lost a grip on a rope and—"

"We're fine." John slowly got up, keeping his hand on his shoulder the whole way. "We should get moving. Longer we stand here, colder we're all going to get."

The prospector hesitated, glancing at me. "You're not hurt?"

"Nothing that won't heal." John offered a tight smile as he carefully rolled his shoulder.

"We're fine," I said. "No harm done."

The man hesitated again, but then nodded and continued up to rejoin his team.

Once we were alone, I turned to John again. "You should've just gotten out of the way."

"That thing could've immobilized our mech."

"And it could've crushed you against it!" I narrowed my eyes. "John, for God's sake, I know you don't want anything happening to your device, but just remember, the damned thing doesn't do anyone any good if you're not around to use it."

He eyed me as he dusted the snow off his trousers. "And a crippled mech won't get the rest of our provisions to the top of the pass."

"No, it won't, but—"

"If the mech had slipped, it would've hit you." He held my gaze. "I wasn't going to let that happen."

I glanced around, and then touched his waist. "Just don't get yourself killed, all right? I'm not going to get very far without you."

"I won't." He brought my hand up and kissed the back of my glove. "We should get moving."

We exchanged a brief look, one that sent a warm tingle through my cold, exhausted body. We didn't dare risk a kiss out here, but that glance alone would hold me over until the next time we had a warm, private place to touch.

I climbed over the mech and took my place behind it again. We switched off the brakes, and the mech resumed its upward climb.

With every step, the ascent became more difficult. I found myself stopping to rest after just four or five steps. Soon, it was every two or three. Even when I stopped to rest, I never quite caught my breath. It wasn't just me either. The other teams huffed and puffed. John stopped to rest as often as I did.

But at long last, we reached the top.

After we'd cleared the final step, I almost dropped to my knees in the snow. There were still plenty of miles between us and Dawson City, but we'd made it to the top of Chilkoot Pass.

John leaned against the mech. "You have to admit—" He paused to take a few breaths. "—it's almost worth it just for the view."

Still panting, my lungs aching and my whole body hurting wherever it wasn't numb, I gazed out at the scenery. John had a point. The snow-covered mountains and forest-blanketed hills were beautiful from here.

I clapped his shoulder. "Yes. *Almost* worth it."

Chapter 18

From the Diary of Dr. Jonathon W. Fauth — October 15, 1898

Though danger still has us warily glancing over our shoulders, Robert and I have left the encampment and at last gained ground on our journey. We've arrived in Canada, thank God. Crossing into it via the Chilkoot Pass was quite the ordeal—mostly uneventful, but hardly an easy ascent.

Oftentimes the tales men tell of places turn out to be nothing more than fanciful exaggerations. London is a fog-choked, congested city, not the glamorous mecca of cosmopolitan society. Likewise, New York and Chicago are cold, crime-riddled places instead of the beating hearts of civilization as many men are led to believe.

As such, I fully anticipated Chilkoot Pass to be far less than what had trickled south by way of stories and rumors. Imagine my surprise then, when we arrived at Chilkoot's foot early yesterday morning. I can testify to anyone who should ever read this—the tales are true. Chilkoot Pass is a monstrous, snow-blanketed peak, and to say its ascent is a daunting task would be to deny it the credit it deserves.

Mangled, half-snowed-over mechs are strewn across the land at the bottom of the pass. Along the trail itself— the fabled Golden Staircase, one and a half thousand steps carved right into the ice for ease of travel—abandoned and crippled mechs dot the terrain like wads of tobacco spit. Those at the bottom are nearly skeletal, having been picked over and stripped clean of any parts that might still be useful. Brass clangs, men curse, animals protest, and mechs slip and slide across the icy ground.

If there was one story of Chilkoot Pass that I am convinced is pure exaggeration, it is the tales of the ease with which mechs whisk provisions over the mountain like a Clydesdale carrying a kitten over a bluff. I firmly believe now that we, like every man en route to Dawson City, were gullibly swindled when we purchased these things.

The dangers of crossing the pass today did offer one benefit, that being relative safety from thieves and bandits. Ever-present Mounties keep a watchful eye over the men making the ascent, and any man on the Golden Staircase would be a fool to be concerned with anything other than keeping his own feet and provisions on the path. We were probably safer out there—from men, at least—than in the encampment this morning.

And now, with our joints aching and our bodies exhausted, we've set up camp in a similar encampment on the other side.

We're in Canada now, the most grueling part of our journey behind us, but I fear there are more dangers ahead than I can even express to Robert. I still worry for his safety. Tomorrow, there will be no more Mounties forming a barrier between us and those who wish to get their hands on my device.

I have no choice but to go on even if it means crossing the lawless no-man's-land outside these rickety gates. I cannot remain in the safety of this encampment forever.

Even if I could, my livelihood—everything I've ever worked for—depends upon making it to the gold fields.

Tomorrow, we go on.

Chapter 19

A stick cracked.

In a heartbeat, John and I were both wide awake and upright. He snatched his pistol from under his pillow. I pulled the rifle out from under the bedroll.

Snow crunched.

Because of the cold and constant danger, we'd slept in our boots, so we scrambled up and darted outside.

For a moment, I thought we'd just been paranoid again, but then a shadow scrambled away from beside the tent.

"Robert, stay there." John lunged at the shadow. It changed direction, sprinting past me, but I swung the rifle and hit him hard in the gut. He doubled over and took a knee.

John grabbed him by the back of his jacket and shoved him all the way to the ground. They grappled, but the intruder quickly freed himself and disappeared into the night.

"Damn," John muttered. "These bastards are getting bolder."

"They are." This was the third attempt in as many nights. I set the rifle at my feet and offered John my arm.

He clasped his hand around my forearm, and once he was on his feet, said, "I suspect this won't get any better between here and the gold fields."

"No, I don't think so." Something twisted beneath my ribs. Though we were nearer to Dawson City with each passing day, the gold fields seemed farther and farther out of our reach. As if the thieves and Sidney's men and the whole damned world were closing in. Sooner or later…

I shook my head and tried not to think of that. The only choices we had were going on or turning back, and neither was safe. Nothing was.

Wincing, John gingerly rubbed his shoulder.

"Still hurts?"

"It'll heal. I'm not concerned." He scowled. "Not about that, anyway."

I glanced at the trail where our would-be thief had gone. "What do we do now? Isn't like we can have the Mounties protect us out here."

"I know."

"Maybe we should sleep in shifts. At least if one of us is awake…"

John nodded. "Good idea. You go ahead and sleep."

"Are you sure?"

"Yes." He squeezed my arm. "I am so sorry, Robert. I knew this would be dangerous, but I brought you into this and—"

I put my gloved hand over his. "I knew what I was getting into when I came back to you in Ketchikan."

"Still." The pad of his thumb drew soft arcs on my sleeve. "I don't want anything to happen to you."

"Likewise. Wake me if you get tired. I doubt I'll be sleeping anyway."

"I will."

I was right—I didn't sleep much. By the time I'd started to drift off, John roused me so he could sleep. I sat outside next to the campfire, a book beside me and the rifle across my lap. A few times, I tried to read to pass the time, but my tired eyes couldn't focus on the printing and my paranoid mind couldn't concentrate on the words. If not for the cold and the constant certainty our campsite was about to be invaded, I'd have nodded off.

Throughout the night, we traded off every hour or two. By dawn, neither of us was well rested, but all we could do was continue down the trail. For the next three nights, it was the same routine—alternating sleeping and watching in between chasing off would-be thieves.

By the third morning, I was so exhausted I could barely move.

John finished his coffee and put the cup in the mech with our other gear. "Ready?"

"Ready."

John lit the boiler, and while we waited for the steam to build pressure, we started taking down the campsite.

As I put our bedrolls onto the mech, I glanced down and froze. A prickling sensation crept down my spine. "Uh, John?"

He looked up from wedging his device between two other boxes. "Hmm?"

"I believe...we have a problem." I gestured at the mech.

"What?" He hurried around the side. "What in the name of..."

Two legs were completely encased in a thick layer of ice.

"How did that happen?" I asked.

"It's sabotage. It must be." He gestured at the icicles and frozen droplets. "Someone's poured water over it."

My stomach twisted. "How did we not hear that?" But the noise all around us answered my question. Crackling fires, snorting horses, barking dogs, groaning mechs, laughing men—the sound of someone pouring water nearby wouldn't have caught his attention or mine.

John swore under his breath. "Well, there's nothing we can do but remove the ice. You work on that one. I'll work on this one."

We melted away the thickest ice with a torch John made out of a stick and a rag, and then chipped away at what was left so we wouldn't damage the joints with the fire.

By the time we'd finished, most of the other teams within sight had broken camp and begun lumbering north. We wouldn't get far today—the days were getting shorter as winter closed in.

Still, any progress was progress, and took us closer to those gold fields. With the mech's legs free of ice, John switched on the engine, and—

Nothing.

Just a hiss of steam beneath the mech's front end, but the engine remained still and quiet.

John knelt and peered under the mech. "Damn!"

"What now?"

He held up the severed ends of the lines connecting the boiler to the engine. "Apparently we're staying here a little while longer."

I swallowed. "How long will it take to fix?"

"Depends on how much damage there is." He glanced at the caravan of teams inching past us. "But we may as well set up camp again."

Chapter 20

From the Diary of Dr. Jonathon W. Fauth — October 17, 1898

More than ever, I question the wisdom of continuing this journey. Multiple times since we've crossed the Chilkoot Pass, thieves have attempted to obtain my device.

This morning, we found our mech sabotaged with ice and a cut line. We repaired it, but it cost us valuable time.

Now, I am truly afraid of every mile between here and Dawson City. These are no longer simple, greedy thieves. Someone is biding his time, slowing us down until we are, as we are now, alone and isolated, immobile out here in the wilderness.

My heart pounds and my hands sweat whenever another team overtakes us on the trail, so certain am I that every man on this route is a potential thief. Neither of us can sleep. As such, we are both terribly weary, and our progress has slowed dramatically.

I've tried again to persuade Robert to move on without me. I can navigate the mech alone if I have to, or we can both shoulder whatever we can carry and go on that way.

Stubborn as a mule, though, he's still here with me. As I write this, he sits just an arm's length from me, his hands hovering over the fire, his eyes tired and his face expressionless. Any sound—a woodland creature, a branch cracking beneath the weight of ice and snow, sap popping in the fire—makes him jump, and his weary eyes immediately come to life, widening and scanning the shadows. Then his shoulders sink again, and his gaze returns to the fire.

My reactions are not unlike his. Every sound, every movement has me seizing the rifle that now leans against my leg, and it takes very little to send us both into panic. I can't imagine how either of us will be able to sleep tonight.

How many days lie ahead, it's impossible to say. I don't imagine last night's sabotage will be the last such effort, but there—

Chapter 21

Something cracked nearby.

John's head snapped up, his journal nearly falling out of his hands and into the fire. "What was that?"

I tensed, searching the darkness for movement. "I don't know. But it was close by."

"I know." His hand casually drifted to the rifle at his side.

We both rose.

The fire at our feet was a double-edged sword. It illuminated our campsite, but deepened the shadows beyond. Firelight glinted off the mech, which we'd parked within sight this time instead of chaining to a tree, but aside from that, we were surrounded by a thick curtain of black.

Another cracking sound turned our heads. John shouldered the rifle, and I rested my hand on the pistol at my hip. Movement behind me caught my attention, but before I could turn, something blunt hit the back of my head. I grunted and dropped, my knee landing hard on the frozen ground.

Pain and disorientation blurred the resulting commotion for a few seconds. When my vision cleared, everything was still, and John stood poised with the rifle up, aimed at someone behind me.

"Get back, or I'll put a bullet through every one of you," he snarled. "Robert, are you all right?"

"I'm fine." Rubbing the back of my head, I staggered to my feet.

"Just give us the device, Dr. Fauth." The voice sent a shiver down my spine. Immediately, I was back on the deck of the steamboat en route to Ketchikan, and my stomach coiled with the same nausea that had driven me outdoors that day in the first place.

"You want a device like this?" John's voice was steady and cold. "Why don't you go back to Sidney and ask him to build one."

"Let's not play games," came the equally steady reply. "With this weather, I think we'd all like to sleep sometime tonight, no?"

"Then get moving. You're not getting this device."

Logan laughed. "Are you really foolish enough to die for your equipment?"

"Are you?" John growled.

"He's bluffing," one of the other men snarled.

"Am I?" John asked.

"I have a better idea," Logan said from behind me.

An instant later, a hand seized the back of my jacket collar and someone kicked my knees out from under me. For the second time in minutes, I hit the ground hard, pain shooting up from my kneecaps. My gun clattered onto the frozen dirt beside me, and a boot toed it out of my reach.

Cold metal pressed against the side of my head.

I froze, staring up at John.

"I'm not asking again, Dr. Fauth," Logan said. The distinctive creak of a hammer drawing back made me gulp. "Give us the device."

John swallowed hard. The rifle's barrel dipped slightly, but he didn't lower the gun all the way. "Let him go."

"Hand over the device."

"Hand him over first."

Aside from my pounding heart and the softly crackling fire, the night was eerily silent. Firelight danced along the rifle barrel and across John's features. His dark eyes were fixed on the man behind me.

"Give us the gold finder." Logan tapped the side of my head with the pistol. "It's him or the device, Dr. Fauth."

John swallowed. My stomach lurched. He'd told me to reconsider traveling with him, never *quite* denying that he'd take a bullet to save his work, but I'd never asked if he'd expect me to take one.

John...

Slowly, John lowered the rifle. "Let him go, and it's yours."

My heart stopped.

The pistol dug into my temple. "The device first."

John hesitated. His eyes shifted from me to the men behind me to me again. Then he nodded, and a second later, disappeared into the tent.

"My, my, he *is* attached to you." Cold gloved fingers stroked my hair, and I couldn't help shuddering.

"Isn't that charming?" another asked. "And to think we all thought that was just a rumor."

"A rumor?" Logan snorted. He trailed a fingertip across the back of my neck along my hairline, his taunting caress contrasting sharply with the ice-cold barrel digging into my temple. "Hardly."

The tent flap moved, and John reappeared, holding the wooden box in one hand and his rifle in the other. "All right. Here it is."

The hand lifted off my neck. "Open the box."

"Let him go, and I'll open it."

"Dr. Fauth, I'm not in the mood to play games." The man jabbed my temple with the gun, making me wince. "Open the box, or I'll open his head."

I gulped. John met my eyes, and the fear in his did nothing to calm me.

He reached into his pocket and withdrew a small key. Kneeling, he laid the rifle by his feet and reached for the box. With the click of the lock, a lump rose in my throat. His entire livelihood, his one chance to complete his research, and he was trading it for my life.

God, I am so sorry, John.

The hinges creaked, and John gestured at the device, which was nestled safely in its padding. "There. Now let him go."

"Step back from it."

John took a step back.

"William," my captor said. "Pick it up."

One of the men stepped forward, closed the box, and picked it up. John watched, his lips twisted with a hundred different emotions. He winced and looked away as the man named William returned to this side of the campsite with the box in hand.

John took a breath. "You have the detector." His voice shook now, though I couldn't tell if it was fear or fury. "Now let him go. We had a deal."

"I've changed my mind." The gun left my temple, and someone hauled me to my feet by the scruff of my jacket. "He's coming with us."

John started to bring up the rifle but paused in midair. From the corner of my eye, I caught the glint of firelight off the barrel of a raised pistol.

"Give it up, Fauth," Logan growled. "He's coming with us. You take one step, he's a dead man."

John stared at him in horror, eyes wide and lips apart. "Why? I gave you what you asked for. Why do you need him? He's not part of this."

"Call it a little insurance," came the reply. "I see you or a Mountie come anywhere near us or this device? He's dead. Now why don't you just go about your business while we continue? Men?" He hauled me back a step. Then another. "Don't cross me, Fauth. I *will* kill him."

I met John's eyes. I'd never imagined it was possible for the man to look so terrified. Or for me to feel this helpless. *Oh God, how do I get out of this?*

"Come on." Logan turned me around and forced me to walk forward. Step-by-step, we headed into the dark of the night, leaving my campsite and my lover behind.

John wasn't ready to give up, though. We'd gone perhaps twenty yards when a gunshot cracked the night's silence, and a bullet whistled past us. Then another.

My captors dived for cover, hauling me down with them. Someone pinned me to the frozen ground. I struggled to withdraw my own pistol, but couldn't get to it.

"Kill the kid, Logan. Fool's opening fire, so shoot the damned kid."

"I have a better idea." The next shot came from right beside me, and was so loud, my vision turned white. Another shot came from the distance, then two more from right beside me, and over the ringing in my ears, I heard a laugh, followed by, "That'll take care of him."

I wrenched away from Logan and looked back.

And immediately wished I hadn't.

The fire backlit John. He was on his knees, wavering badly. Then he slumped forward and crumpled to the ground.

I heard myself cry out his name, I felt the tears sting my eyes, but everything was so far away. Like I was outside myself, standing off to the side and watching myself collapse with grief as these men, these thieves and murderers, hauled me to my feet and dragged me north while John's blood soaked the snow behind them.

I couldn't say how long we trudged through the still, icy night before they steered off the main road—if one could call it that—down a narrow side trail. Perhaps ten yards down that trail, we came to a campsite.

The men stripped me of the gun I'd carried in my pocket, then sat me unceremoniously beside a dark fire pit. They lit a fire, and I couldn't even feel the heat coming off it. Nor could I taste the food they insisted I eat. I was just...numb.

And though they kept me warm and fed, it didn't take them long to start debating my fate.

"Why even bother keeping him with us?" William asked. "Fauth is dead. This kid's just a liability now."

"No," Logan said coolly. "He's a liability if we let him go."

"Who said anything about letting him go?" The third man asked. "Men turn up dead out here all the time. Nothing unusual." He watched me over the fire, eyes narrowed and icy, and I shivered.

"We're not murderers," Logan said. "Fauth? We were defending ourselves. This one?" He gestured at me. "Well, the machine'll find the gold, but we need someone to dig it up, don't we?"

"Hold on now." The third put up his hands. "We're supposed to be taking this thing back to Chicago, not going north."

Logan nodded. "But after all this cold and ice nonsense, I think we've earned ourselves a trip to the gold fields." He grinned, the flickering fire adding sinister shadows to his face. "We ain't expected back anytime soon, after all."

"Do you know how to use the device?" William asked.

Logan shrugged. "Can't be so complicated, can it? And anyhow, it's got drawings and whatnot with it. If it can get us to the gold, we'll damn sure figure it out."

William scratched at his beard. "And it'll really find gold?"

"That's what Sidney told me. It finds some sorts of metal, and one of 'em is gold."

The other men exchanged glances.

Logan clapped my knee. "And besides. He was heading that way anyway. Weren't you, lad?"

They all looked at me. I stared into the fire and pretended their laughter didn't turn my stomach.

Something told me I wasn't going to live through this.

~*~

After a long day of walking beside my captors' mech, I could barely take another step. My body was cold. My feet, knees, and back ached. My face was wind-burned and my fingers numb, but none of this compared to the deep, burning grief in my chest.

Though I was dead on my feet and even deader inside, the men ordered me to help set up the tents. Once the tents were pitched, it was my task to move certain provisions inside from the mech to keep them safe from thieves and snow. I did as I was told only because the sooner I did what they asked, the sooner they'd let me eat and get warm by the fire. To that end, they'd been kind enough; whenever they stopped to eat, I was allowed food and warmth as well. Couldn't let their newly acquired servant starve or freeze, after all.

At last, it was time for us all to bed down. Logan and Michael took one tent. William ordered me into the other tent with him.

He put his bedroll beside the tent flap and kept a rifle at his side. They didn't bother binding me—where could I go? I'd only just warmed up after my long, cold walk. I had no provisions beyond the coat on my back and a small wad of money in my pocket. Money that was all but useless out here. And this far north, only a fool would take for granted the kindness of passing strangers. Not when their own provisions dwindled and they were *this close* to the gold they sought.

But my captors overestimated my fear of the Canadian winter. And perhaps they overestimated my sanity as well. Let the cold kill me, let a bear find me, let a bandit cut my throat, but I wasn't staying with these men. I'd take my chances against the elements.

I waited until I was certain William was asleep. Then, moving as stealthily as I could, willing my teeth not to chatter and give me away, I got up. I leaned over him and pulled the tent flap back. Everyone else was asleep, and the fire had been doused. Perfect.

I held my breath and stepped over William. He didn't move a muscle, didn't even stir in his sleep, and in seconds, I was out of the tent and in the bitter, biting cold.

Thank you, Father, for teaching me to hunt in the snow. If there was one thing I could do, it was creep through snow as stealthily as the various animals my brothers and I hunted with our father in the wilds of Montana. Without making a sound, I made it to the perimeter of the campsite, and there, I stopped and looked back. The frozen ground crunched with the shifting of my weight.

John's device was still in the camp. Though it was useless to me, I could get it back to the university where he'd worked. Or...something. I'd sort that out when I was safely back in civilization. For now, I couldn't bear the thought of the invention that had driven John this far, right to his death, remaining in their possession.

But how could I get it back? I didn't know where it was held, and I was unarmed.

I resisted the urge to groan as the truth set in: If I wanted to save the device, I needed to plan my escape. I couldn't do it tonight.

Cursing under my breath, I backtracked. I returned to the camp, brushed the snow off my boots, pushed the tent flap aside, and crept over William once more. I eased myself onto my bedroll and pulled the thin blanket up over me.

For the rest of the night, I stared at the inside of the tent and ran through every possible escape plan I could come up with that allowed me to leave with John's device.

"Whatever it takes, John," I vowed into the stillness. "They won't get rich off your invention and your blood."

Chapter 22

My third night in captivity, I was ready to make my escape. Walking beside the mech each day, I'd taken a careful inventory of their provisions. I knew exactly what I needed, and where it was all stored. At night, the men only kept a few things from the mech in the safety of their tents: Food, guns, coal...and the locked wooden box. Everything else stayed in the mech, and after rehearsing my movements in my mind and counting my steps when I carried the food and coal into their tent each night, I knew precisely how quickly I could get everything I needed.

The routine each time was the same: Once I'd moved everything they'd ordered me to move, Logan would send me to sit beside the campfire with the others. Then, and only then, he'd take the locked box into the tent.

That was the one hitch in my plan. The tent was cramped, there were other boxes and crates stacked inside it, and it would be dark. I wouldn't have much time to get in, find and retrieve the box, and get out.

Lying in my bedroll, I listened for William's breathing to fall into its pattern of sleep. It didn't take long, fortunately. Every one of us was exhausted, myself included. Had he taken another ten minutes to fall asleep, I'd have drifted off myself and had to wait another night to make my run.

As soon as I was sure he was asleep, I crept out of my bedroll just like I did the other night. At least this part I'd rehearsed; I knew I could get past him, out of the tent, and beyond the camp's perimeter without detection. It was the rest of the plan I wasn't so sure about.

Outside the tent, I stopped and listened. Quiet snoring came from the other tent, but otherwise, everyone and everything was still. I crept across the campsite to the mech, which was beside the other tent. Closer than I was comfortable with, but it would have to do.

It took less than a minute to gather everything on the list in my mind: matches, an empty flour sack, and a can of gunpowder. I moved my tiny cache a few paces away from the campsite so no one would hear if I made some noise.

The gunpowder can took a little work to pry open, and when the lid finally came off, my heart stopped. The resulting pop seemed to echo all along the silent trail, but after a full minute, no one had responded. I released my breath and went back to my task.

Muffling the sound as much as I could, I tore a few strips off the flour sack and tucked them into my pocket. Then I poured most of the gunpowder into the sack. Moving stealthily, I picked everything up and tiptoed back into the campsite. I laid the torn strips on top of various provisions—whatever was most likely to burn—and sprinkled a thin layer of gunpowder all over everything. Then I put the entire sack on one end of the mech, beside the boiler and steam engine.

Then I dug some wire out of the bag of tools and wound it tightly around each of the mech's three relief valves. Using embers from the fire, I lit the boiler. The engine was still switched off, but soon the boiler would slowly—and more or less quietly—build up pressure.

With everything in place and the water slowly beginning to boil, I took a few deep breaths. I mentally mapped out the distance from here to the tent a few times, making sure I had plenty of time.

I only had one chance, and it was too late to turn back now.

One more deep breath. One struck match. One, two, three burning strips of flour sack. As the flames inched toward the first deposits of gunpowder, I dropped the matches into the mech and ran to the opposite side of the tent, slipping and sliding on the icy ground. It didn't matter if anyone heard me now; they were about to be occupied with *much* more pressing matters.

I stopped beside the tent and waited.

Just as I'd hoped, the fire met the gunpowder. It started out as a few quiet pops, but as the fire spread, the gunpowder exploded with more force, and in seconds, both tents were alive with voices and activity.

The three men scrambled to put out the fire, and I darted into the tent Michael and Logan had occupied. I felt around, squinted in the darkness, heart thundering in my chest as I searched for the box.

"Come on, come on, where is it?" I murmured under my breath. I shoved aside bedrolls, bags, furs, everything. Damn it, where was it?

Then everything went wrong.

The boiler exploded with more force than I'd expected. The tent listed with the blast, but then something landed on top of it. My heart jumped into my throat. Whatever it was—a box or a crate, I supposed— was on fire. I had only seconds before it would burn through the top of the tent.

"Shit," I muttered. I frantically felt around. No way was I leaving without this thing. No way, I'd come too far, I'd—

There.

I snatched the box out from under the bags of coal.

Fabric ripped. I barely had time to shield my face as a flaming crate fell through the top of the tent, knocking me off-balance. I went to my knees, dropping the box. As I hurried back to my feet and reached for the box again, another explosion sent more debris into the air, and it rained down through the gaping, flaming hole in the tent. Something landed on my collar, and in an instant, my neck and jaw were ablaze with pure, white hot agony.

I batted at the flames and, a second too late, realized I'd cried out.

"Hey! He's in the tent!" Logan's voice echoed over the raging fire. Someone lunged in and grabbed for me, but I kicked his hands away. I seized the device's box and darted past him. He tried to snatch my arm, and this time I swung the box into the side of his head, knocking him flat. He didn't get up, but the other two men were still on their feet.

"Shoot him!" William's voice boomed through the night. "He's got the detector! Shoot him!"

I ran. I ran like hell. I ran like the frigid air didn't make my lungs ache, and my bones weren't ready to splinter from the cold, and my face didn't burn like fire. I veered off the road into the thick forest. Running blind, I wove between trees, staying low when I could, and every time I was sure I couldn't take another step, a bullet ricocheted off a tree or whistled past, and I kept running.

I snagged my foot on an upraised root, and both the box and I went flying. I landed hard, biting back another cry as my ankle twisted and my burned flesh smacked the frozen ground.

More gunshots. Shouts. Footsteps.

Twigs snapped beneath feet. The moonlight illuminated William's face and glittered across the rifle in his hands. Far too close for comfort, he turned his head left, right, left, and I prayed he didn't look down. Some underbrush obscured me, but the moon could still pick me out like it had him.

I held my breath and held still, willing myself to stay silent in spite of the relentless pain. I clenched my jaw to keep my teeth from chattering, but I shivered so badly from cold, fear, and pain, I was sure the rustling of my jacket would give me away.

Then he stopped and shook his head. Cursing, he turned and left. I released my breath but waited to move until his footsteps had faded into the night. Then I gave it a few more minutes just to be sure he hadn't come back, or that Michael hadn't come after me himself.

Finally, when I was certain I was alone, I dragged myself over to the box and just held it to my chest. There was no guarantee I'd survive this, especially not out here alone in the damned Yukon, but at least I had John's device away from his murderers.

Cold comfort if there ever was.

~*~

Walking. Walking. Endless fucking walking.

With the daylight came other teams, thank God. One stopped me and insisted on letting me warm myself by their fire. Bland barely cooked beans had never tasted so good.

One member of the team also offered bandages for the burn on my face, and in the semi-reflective surface of a gold pan, I got to see how badly I'd been burned. My stomach twisted and turned as I examined the angry red spanning one side of my throat from my collarbone all the way up and over my jaw.

So much for my former profession.

But I was alive. Alive, and with John's device in my possession, so I *had* to go on.

Fed and warmed, I continued south while the others all went north. Each night, I managed to find a team who'd let me bed down, and each morning, I'd keep going.

All along the trail were the remains of campsites. Smoldering fire pits, dots of tobacco spit, the flattened spot where a tent had been.

One abandoned campsite was different from all the others, though. I came across it after three days, and halted. An abandoned mech stood, stripped bare of both provisions and parts, beside a black circle that had once been a campfire. It didn't seem much different from the others aside from the mech, but a sick feeling in my heart told me it was.

It was *our* campsite. Well, what was left of it.

Nothing remained except the skeletal mech. The tent, the rifle, the bedrolls, all of it had been taken. Even John's books and his beloved journal were gone.

And so was John. All that remained of him was a pool of blood. Crimson, frozen blood, and far, far too much of it spread across the snow. I was torn between turning away before I got sick, and kneeling to touch it, if only for one last macabre connection to him.

I dropped to my knees. Exhaustion and grief took over, and I...I couldn't take another step. I tried not to imagine what had happened to him, if some wild animal had gotten to him or if a passing team stopped to bury him. If they had, I was grateful, because I couldn't have buried him out here. Even if the ground weren't frozen solid, I had no shovels or pickaxes left, and there was neither fuel nor matches to burn him.

But it didn't matter, because his body was gone.

I hugged the wooden box to my chest and tried to stop crying, if only because the tears seeped under the bandages and stung the burn on my face.

You can do this, Robert. There's no one else on this earth who can get this device back to Chicago. Get up and walk, damn you.

I gave the abandoned campsite a long look. Although our last moments together in this place had been hellish, leaving wasn't easy. The camp hadn't yielded a single keepsake, not even his journal, and so I had nothing left of John. Nothing except my memories and the device. Once I moved on, there'd be nothing more. He was gone. Forever.

But if I stayed here, I'd freeze to death, and John's device would never make it home.

Swallowing hard, I carefully wiped away my tears, then pushed myself to my feet, wavering slightly on exhausted legs. I turned south. The road seemed to stretch on for thousands and thousands of miles, and Chilkoot Pass was so far in the distance. How I'd get back over it, I didn't know, but I had no choice.

I took a step.

Then another.

And I kept walking.

Chapter 23

The bandages were soaked through with sweat by the end of the second day, stinging the burn and freezing solid around the edges. I pulled them off and threw them aside, cringing as the burning worsened now that the wound was exposed to the air. The cold wind stung my face, but covering the burn meant my jacket stuck to the wounded flesh. I spent half the time trying to keep one side of my face warm, and the other half stopping to put snow against the burned skin.

My ankle still ached a little from twisting it in my escape, but I wasn't completely lame, and for that I was thankful. There were enough miles ahead without limping every step.

As I walked, I tried to keep my mind on anything but John's death or the cold or the pain in my neck and face. The future seemed as good a thing as any to focus on because the present left me angry and devastated.

Once I made it back to Skagway or Juneau, I could find transportation to Ketchikan, and from there, a steamboat back to Seattle. Paying for such a thing wouldn't be easy. The thin wad of dollars left in my pocket wouldn't get me far, and I tried not to think of how I'd earn more money to make the journey or how I'd survive at all after I reached Seattle. My previous profession had likely gone up in flames; my only hope there would be men who were desperate enough for another man to overlook a badly scarred face.

Injury or not, though, I *had* to find some other means of making money. Now that I had known John's touch, I couldn't bring myself to sell my own.

John. Oh God, John. It was just as well I couldn't stop to sleep, because every time I closed my eyes, I relived that moment when John, backlit by our glowing campfire, crumpled into the snow.

Flinching at the memory, I shook my head, and immediately regretted it when the movement stretched my burned skin. The resulting pain brought back everything that had happened when I'd escaped. And my imprisonment. And my kidnapping. And John's death.

Again and again, time after time, my mind went back to that moment when he was gone from me, and though my grief threatened to drive me to the ground, my anger kept me going. One way or another, I was getting to that encampment with John's device.

A steady stream of stampeders passed me on their way north. Some offered me warmth, food, and bandages, others just eyed me and kept moving. At least a dozen teams had pack horses and mules, but no amount of begging and offering every penny I had would persuade them to sell me one of their animals. Even those who had mechs refused to spare a horse. I understood; with as much as every man had to carry, any beast or machine of burden was worth keeping.

Shortly before daylight faded into night, I came across a team setting up camp.

One of the stampeders looked at me and did a double take. "Lord, what happened to your face, son?"

I tucked my chin self-consciously, though it wouldn't hide the majority of the burn. "Long story. I don't suppose I can beg a night by your fire?"

"Of course, of course." He gestured toward their campfire. Then he extended his hand. "I'm Edgar."

"Robert," I whispered, and shook his hand.

He looked me up and down, eyes pausing on the box I held in my numb hand. "You out here by yourself? No provisions at all? Were you robbed or something?"

I pursed my lips. "You could say that."

The other stampeder stepped out of the tent, and Edgar gestured at me. "Robert, this is Jimmy."

Jimmy looked at me, and his eyebrows jumped. "My Lord, what's happened to you?"

They showed me to the campfire, and as I thawed my frozen hands and feet, Jimmy passed me a whiskey flask. Then they waited for me to explain my wounds and my lack of provisions. I moistened my lips, drew a breath, and told them what had happened.

When I'd finished, I took a long drink. Then I swept the back of my sleeve across my lips, and before they could ask questions I didn't have the energy to answer, I nodded toward their two pack horses. "How much for one of your horses?"

They glanced at each other, then at me.

"Pardon me, son?" Jimmy asked.

I moistened my lips. "I'll never make it back to Chilkoot Pass on foot. If I can ride, maybe I can make it."

They exchanged another look. Edgar nodded.

Jimmy turned to me. "Fifty dollars."

I blinked. "Fifty dollars? I could buy three good pack horses for half that."

"And there's no one selling horses up this way," Edgar said.

"You have a mech," I said through my teeth. "I'll give you thirty-five for the horse."

Another look passed between them, and this time Jimmy nodded.

Edgar leaned his hands on his knees. "Forty-five."

"Forty."

"Deal."

I exhaled. That was almost my last dollar. If I needed more than that, I'd have to earn it. Somehow. But that could be dealt with when I made it to Ketchikan. For now, expensive or not, this horse was the only thing that could get me to the encampment by the Chilkoot before I collapsed from sheer exhaustion. If I had to let a man fuck me for a few dollars to get anywhere after that, so be it. I just didn't want to think about what kind of man would be desperate enough to bed me now.

I tried not to glare at Edgar and Jimmy. They'd been kind enough to give me food, rest, whiskey, and warmth. Wasn't every man on this journey greedy in his own way? There was no sense begrudging them trying to get every last dollar I had in exchange for their horse—at least they'd been willing to sell me the damn thing. They could have just sent me on my way on foot.

They also offered to let me bed down in their camp for the night. For that alone, I could forgive them for lightening my pockets by more dollars than I could spare.

~*~

The horse was worth the money and then some. When I could barely hold myself upright, the horse kept walking, and even when I slumped over her neck and struggled to stay awake, we gained ground. I kept one arm around the box, and it bit into my stomach whenever I leaned over it, but hell if I was going to drop it. Not after I'd made it this far.

Hours and miles both crawled past. No new snow fell, but the temperature dropped. The snow beneath her hooves was frozen solid and treacherously slick, and I shivered inside my thick—but not nearly thick enough—jacket. It was all I could do to stay on the mare's back. Just holding the reins in one hand and the wooden box in the other took every bit of concentration and energy I had, and between pain, exhaustion, and cold, I was close to delirious.

So close, in fact, I refused to believe my eyes when they told me the Chilkoot Pass was as close as it looked. Or that there was a flag up ahead. A red flag whipping in the wind. A red flag with the Union Jack in its upper corner and a yellow coat of arms off to the side. On a tall wooden pole. Above a ramshackle log cabin that looked an awful lot like the North-West Mounted Police outposts on either side of the pass.

But the hallucination didn't fade. With every step, the colors became brighter. More vivid. More…real.

I blinked. Squinted. Stared.

It was real. And so was the building below it, and the tents behind it, and…

I'd made it. Relieved tears stung my eyes. I'd finally made it.

Clutching the box closer to me, I steered the horse toward the encampment.

Dozens of teams were crowded outside with their mechs and animals, and a trio of Mounties checked over their papers to make sure everything was still in order from their pre-pass inspection. A couple of heads turned my way. Then a few more. One of the Mounties looked up, furrowing his brow at me. He handed some papers back to a stampeder and started across the frozen ground toward me.

"You all right, son?" he asked.

I was tired of that question, but coming from a Mountie, it was more than welcome. It meant I was here.

"Son?" He cocked his head and came closer. When I halted the mare, he put a hand on her neck. "What are you

doing out here alone without any provisions? Are you—"
He squinted. "Your face is—"

"Burned. Yes, I know."

He didn't ask if I needed help. He took the mare's reins and led her toward the outpost, and I just closed my eyes and buried the unwounded side of my face against her warm neck while I clung to the wooden box. Voices murmured all around me, and the Mountie leading my horse barked an order to someone else.

The mare halted. I sat up, pushing myself off her neck with one shaking arm as the other kept the box close to me.

The Mountie tied my horse, then reached for the box. "Why don't you let me take that so you can dismount?"

I hesitated.

He beckoned with both hands. "Just until you're off the horse, son. I don't want you falling and hurting yourself."

He had a point. After another moment's hesitation, I carefully lowered the device to him, and he handed it off to another Mountie.

I dismounted, and as soon as my feet hit the ground, my knees collapsed under me. I nearly tumbled to the ground beside the mare, but a Mountie grabbed my arm to steady me. Once I was more or less on my feet, he pulled my arm around his shoulders and helped me into the outpost.

The Mountie eased me into a chair beside the hearth, and I closed my eyes, savoring the warmth and the relief of not being out on that damned trail for a moment longer. Plenty of miles remained ahead of me before I made it back to Seattle, but this part was over.

Something wooden scraped on the hard floor, and when I opened my eyes, more relief swept over me: the box. How many times I almost dropped that thing, I couldn't count, but it was here with me. Out of the hands of John's murderers. One step closer to his university, where it would hopefully be put to use in his good name.

The Mountie who'd helped me into the room sat in another chair.

"Thanks for the help." My throat was raw from the cold. "I thought I was seeing things when I saw your flag."

"No, you weren't. But what on earth were you doing out there with nothing?"

"I was robbed," I whispered.

"And the rest of your team?"

I swallowed hard, wincing as much from the memory as the pain in my throat. "Dead."

His chair creaked. He rested his elbows on his knees and eyed me intently. "How far have you come alone?"

"I…" I licked my dry lips and shook my head, wincing again when my face burned. Sooner or later, I'd remember not to do that. "I don't remember. I've been out there for a few days."

The two Mounties exchanged surprised looks. "And you survived?"

"Apparently I did," I said dryly. "I had some help along the way. Teams that let me camp with them." I nodded toward the door. "Sold me the horse."

"Thank God for that," the first Mountie said quietly. "What's your name?"

"Robert." I licked my lips again. "Robert Belton."

He blinked and sat up straight. "I…beg your pardon?"

"My name is Robert Belton," I croaked.

He looked at the other Mountie, something unspoken passing between them.

The second picked up some weathered pages off a table and skimmed over them. He flipped to another page, then another, and his eyebrows jumped. He glanced at his counterpart and gave a sharp nod.

Then he looked at me. "Do you know a"—he glanced at the papers in front of him—"Dr. Jonathon Fauth?"

The mention of his name sent a wave of crushing grief right through me. I closed my eyes. "I did, yes."

"I thought so." He laughed softly and shook his head. "He'll be thrilled to hear you're—"

"What?" My eyes flew open. "What do you mean?"

He stared at me, then gestured over his shoulder. "He's had half this camp scouring—"

I lunged toward him and grabbed his shoulders, digging my fingers in when my balance faltered. "He's here? He's alive?"

"Well, yes." The Mountie helped me back into my chair before I lost what was left of my balance. "He's wounded, but he's been here a couple of days now."

"Take me to him," I pleaded. "Please. I thought he was dead. I was sure of it. He was shot, and—"

"Definitely the same man. Came in here the other day with a bullet in his chest. Half-frozen, nearly bled to death. Another day out there, he wouldn't have made it, I'm certain."

"But…he's all right?"

"He's alive, yes." The Mountie pursed his lips. "He won't be in fighting shape for a time, but…"

My heart beat faster. "Can I see him?"

He put up a hand. "I think we ought to get some food in you, and—"

"I'm fine. I *have* to see him. Now."

They looked at each other, and both shrugged. As they rose, the first offered a hand to help me to my feet.

They were probably right. I was too long without a decent meal and a moment's rest, and my head spun as soon as I was upright. If John was here and alive, he still would be in half an hour's time. But I couldn't wait. I wouldn't. I needed to see him with my own eyes. I needed to be absolutely sure he was really alive. I picked up the box and, although I was certain this was all another delirious dream—I'd had plenty the last couple of restless nights—followed the Mounties out of the outpost and into the encampment.

Walking between rows of tents and mechs and weary men was strange. Surreal. I remembered the fatigue that seeped all the way into the bones and could nearly drive a grown man to weeping like a child. The day we'd arrived here after crossing the Chilkoot, I couldn't have imagined there existed a deeper, more taxing level of exhaustion like that which weighed down on me now. Or that there would ever come a day when a tent, a mech, and a campfire would be even more luxurious than those baths in which we'd indulged on the other side of the pass.

And I certainly never could have imagined the grief I'd experienced over the last few days, or this relief that I begged and begged and *begged* to be real. *Please don't let this be a dream. Please, please, let him really be alive.*

At the other end of the encampment, a large tent stood between the outfitters and the makeshift saloon. Inside that tent, thick curtains hung between beds much like they had between the baths in the other camp, and a nurse wandered from one bed to the next. A boiler rattled and rumbled outside, and a pipe poured enough warm air into the tent to make it almost stuffy.

The Mountie pulled the nurse aside and murmured something to her. She nodded and went to one of the beds, of which only the footboard was visible to me.

"Dr. Fauth?" she said, and my heart jumped into my throat.

"Yes?" That single word instantly brought tears to my eyes. His voice was weak, hoarse, but still somehow cognac smooth. He was alive. He really was.

"How are you feeling?" she asked.

"Same as ever." His tone was flat and vaguely slurred, but *alive*.

She looked toward us and nodded. The Mountie nudged me. I took a deep breath and started toward her. I stepped around the curtain, and for a long, long moment—though perhaps it only spanned a heartbeat or two—I just…stared.

John sat upright on a cot, a white bandage sticking out from beneath the collar of his mostly buttoned shirt. Stubble darkened his jaw, and heavy shadows under his eyes spoke of little to no sleep. His journal slipped from his shaking hands and fell into his lap.

"Robert? Are you…" He shook his head and blinked a few times. To the nurse, he said, "Please tell me I'm not hallucinating again."

I laughed, and a couple of tears made it onto my cheeks. I sniffed sharply and wiped them away as I crossed the short expanse of space to his bedside. "If you are, then so am I."

I sat on the edge of his bed, and he reached up to touch my face but drew his hand back. "What's happened to you? Your skin, it…"

"It's just a burn. It'll heal."

The nurse cleared her throat. "Dr. Fauth, if you need anything else, just call me."

"Thank you." When we were alone, John faced me again. "What happened?"

"It's nothing. I couldn't let them keep your device, so I…" I gestured at the burns.

"My…" He stared blankly at me. "You did this? To save my device?"

"It was your life's work. I couldn't let them keep it."

His eyes widened even more, and he caressed the unwounded side of my face. "Robert…"

I smiled at him. "I'm glad you're all right."

"I'm glad you're all right too, but this…" He touched my chin and gently turned my head, brow furrowing as he inspected my burns. "Oh, Robert. I am so sorry. I never wanted…My work is important, but I never wanted this."

I put my hand over his and kissed his palm. "I had to try."

"No. You…" He winced and shook his head. Then he carefully took my hand in both of his, grimacing at the movement before he brought my fingers up to his lips and kissed them gently. "It took watching them take you away for me to realize it wasn't that damned box I should've been protecting all this time." He kissed my fingers again, and when our eyes met, his were wet. "From that moment on, all I've been able to think about is you. I'd…I'd forgotten about anything except you."

I smirked in spite of the threat of tears. "So I could have just left this damned thing behind?"

He laughed and wiped his eyes. Turning serious again, he touched my face. "As long as you made it back here, you could have dismantled it and burned it for all I give a damn."

"Now you tell me." I set it on the floor beside his bed, then sat up and leaned toward him. "I still can't believe you're alive."

He wrapped an arm around me and kissed me gently. "I can't believe you're here. And alive. And…" He ran his fingers through my hair. "I just can't believe it."

I kissed him and drew it out for a long moment. I didn't care if the nurse or the Mounties or anyone saw us.

As I sat up, he asked, "How did you get away?"

I took a breath and told him what happened. Then he told me about the four teams that passed him by, refusing to stop and help him in spite of his obvious wounds, and the fifth that fed him, sheltered him, and brought him back here on their mech. Even now, listening to him tell the story while he squeezed my hand and reassured me that he was *real*, I could barely believe everything that had transpired. That we'd both made it back here alive.

"Have you had anyone examine your face?" he asked. "Make certain it's—"

"It's fine. I don't imagine it'll get much worse than it was the first night."

"Still." He pursed his lips. "Promise me you'll let one of the nurses look you over?"

"Of course." I dropped my gaze and clasped his hand in mine. Neither of us spoke for a long moment, but then I looked at him again. "So what happens now?"

He gestured at his chest. "I'm not going anywhere for a while, I'm afraid. I don't see myself continuing on to Dawson City."

"But you've already made it this far. You've said yourself your entire livelihood depends on all this."

"I won't be in any condition to travel up that way any time soon. I certainly can't swing a pickax or…" He trailed off and shrugged. "But even if I could, I can't go alone, and I can't ask you to go up there again. It's just too dangerous."

"But…the platinum…your work…"

John shook his head. "I could have found a mountain of platinum up there, and I'd have regretted it 'til the day I died, because that damned device"—he gestured at the box on the floor—"almost cost me the one thing I just can't lose, Robert."

I held his gaze, even as my vision blurred. "But your work…"

"I'll find other ways to do my research." His eyes darted toward the box, and he shrugged with one shoulder. "Maybe I'll just stay in Chicago and manufacture those damned things." He trailed the backs of his fingers down my cheek. "The only thing that matters to me now is you."

My heart jumped. "What happened to wanting to revolutionize communication?"

"Oh, it'll happen. Maybe someday people will be able to see each other's faces and hear each other's voices down a wire." He kissed me lightly. "But if I can't see yours, then what does it matter?"

"John…"

"Let Sidney, Tesla, and Edison beat me to innovation. I just can't lose you." He swallowed hard and held my gaze. "I love you, Robert."

Smiling, I blinked back tears. "I love you too."

He tugged at my shirt and drew me down to kiss him again. When he broke the kiss, he murmured, "I don't suppose I can persuade you to come to Chicago with me, can I?"

I sniffed sharply and batted a tear from my cheek. "I thought you said that city was windy and polluted and all of that."

"It is. But it might be more conducive to making a living than Seattle."

"Good point." I chewed my lip. "Do you…are you sure you want me coming back with you? You know, immoral conduct and all of that?"

He waved a hand. "Let people talk."

"Even if they find out I'm a whore?"

John pulled me closer to him. "You're no man's whore," he whispered, his lip brushing mine. "You're just…"

"Yours." I kissed him and carefully sank into his embrace. "I'm all yours."

"And I'm yours," he whispered. "I love you, Robert."

"I love you too."

Holding on to him just then, both of us weary and wounded, I hadn't an ounce of regret that I'd never made it to Dawson City. I'd left Seattle a whore, returned burned and penniless to Chilkoot, and never once put a pickax to the Yukon's frozen tundra.

But there wasn't a man alive who came back richer from the Klondike Gold Rush.

Epilogue

From the Diary of Dr. Jonathon W. Fauth,
Proprietor, Fauth Prospecting Equipment Company,
Chicago, Illinois — June 17, 1899

The company's profits have been soaring lately. It's remarkable, really. But ever since word came down that they've found gold in Nome, Alaska, everyone still in Dawson City is flocking to Nome, and a new stampede has begun. The timing could not have been more perfect, coming just a month after the second factory opened to manufacture the AR912 Gold Detectors. With the second factory, we are keeping up on orders but barely. I foresee a third facility opening soon.

I've sent a hand-picked team to Seattle, and from there, they will venture up to Nome to test for platinum. Another team is already two weeks into their journey to Dawson City for the same reason. I expect the fields to be picked clean of gold, but I'm holding out hope that there is still a vein or two of platinum left to be found. Then perhaps I can resume my semiconductor work in earnest.

I won't be making the journey this time myself, though. I have my company to run, and Robert has his studies.

Yes, his studies. Since the last time I wrote—my Lord, it's been some time—I'm delighted that he's finally been admitted to the university, though it was a battle for a few months. My former colleagues and superiors were anything but enthusiastic about admitting him. Word had gotten around that his lover is a man—this man in particular. Then newspapers from Ketchikan to Seattle made their way to Chicago with their repeated and emphatic mentions that the man who'd bravely saved my device was a lowly prostitute. He is clearly as intelligent and ambitious as any pupil should be, if not more so, but excuse after excuse had been made to deny him entrance.

Then I met with the dean, and in light of a substantial contribution from Fauth Prospecting to the university's destitute science department, Robert's "immoral conduct" was suddenly not so unpalatable. I generally don't believe a student should be admitted through bribery, but I also don't believe he should be denied entrance based on anything besides his academic performance. I did what needed to be done. It's the least I can do for him.

Since the gatekeepers let him into the academic world, Robert has flourished. Already, the head of the history department is trying to persuade him to consider concentrating his studies there. Several times, he's hinted to Robert about staying at the university even after he graduates. Seems one of the history professors will be retiring in the next several years, and there will be a position available. Professor Robert Belton. I think it has a nice ring to it.

Sometimes I still have to stop and shake my head at how events transpired after I stepped off the train in Seattle less than a year ago. I was probably among the few who left for Dawson City without the faintest aspiration of striking it rich, at least not until I returned to Chicago and finished my work. Strange how things turned out, isn't it?

To this day, Robert still makes my breath catch just like he did the moment I laid eyes on him in that ramshackle Seattle saloon. He's still certain I'll be repulsed by the scarring on his face and neck, but my only revulsion to that scar is knowing how close I came to losing him. How much he risked in order to rescue *my* work.

Most of the time, though, I don't even notice the scars. He's just as bewitching as he was the day I met him. In fact, he's the reason I've been remiss in keeping my journal updated with any kind of regularity. It's difficult to spend much time writing a diary in bed when one is sharing that bed with a lover like Robert, wouldn't you agree?

In fact, I hear him coming down the hall, so I'll end this entry now. I will simply have to wait until tomorrow to write my musings about the next generation detector and a thought I had earlier about how to make them more compact. I have more important things to address for now, outside of my journal.

~*~

John closed his journal as I shut the door behind me. He set the book on the bedside table and laid his pen beside it.

"Working in bed again?" I clicked my tongue as I climbed under the covers with him. "All work and no play, John."

"No play?" He ran his fingers through my hair. "Since when?"

"It's nearly ten o'clock." I draped my arm over his waist and slid closer. "And you're still working."

"I'm not working now."

"But you were working *in bed*." I eyed him playfully. "Again."

He put up a hand and shook his head. "I was doing no such thing. Just chronicling my thoughts for the day."

"All about semiconductors and detectors, yes?"

A hint of amusement flickered across his face, but then he leaned in and kissed me. Gently nudging me onto my back, John murmured, "Semiconductors and detectors, of course," and kissed me again.

He pushed himself up and met my eyes. His fingers drifted down the side of my face, brushing over the scar, but neither he nor I flinched. It hadn't scarred as badly as I'd thought it would—it was unavoidably visible, and still made me cringe whenever I saw it in a mirror, but John hardly noticed it. Scarred or not, once we'd both healed enough to make love again, nothing had changed at all. He didn't shy away from my face any more than I shied away from the scar on his chest. The healed bullet wound simply reminded me of how close I'd come to losing him, and it made me kiss him harder, hold him tighter, and draw out every moment we had in bed.

Small wonder we barely got anything else done.

He ran his fingers through my hair. "You know, I've only just sent the team to Nome to look into platinum deposits up there. Maybe once they've set up camp, we should join them. Get that gold rush experience we never had."

I laughed. "Let them have their adventure. I believe I've quite happily had my fill."

"Hmm." He pursed his lips. "So if I mentioned we might investigate some deposits in Western Australia, you—"

"Australia?" I grinned. "Now, if you send a team *there*, I insist on going too."

"I thought you might." He kissed me gently and barely broke away enough to murmur, "I'll be certain to include us both on that team."

"You most certainly will. Absolutely no way you're going to Australia and leaving me here."

"Robert." He raised his head. "Do you honestly believe I could leave you here? I'd make it as far as New York before I had to come back."

"Good." I grinned.

He pulled me closer and pressed his hips against mine, sucking in a breath when his erection brushed over my own. "Of course I'll take you with me. Anywhere I go." His lips met mine, and the conversation was over. I wrapped my arms around him, and when his hard cock rubbed against mine through our nightclothes, I moaned into his kiss. Why we bothered getting dressed for bed, I didn't know. Nine nights out of ten, we awoke wearing nothing but sheets and each other.

I didn't care where we went, whether we made it to Australia or London or any of the countless places we planned to travel. I had my studies and a possible career as a professor. I had the love of my life.

Indeed, regardless of the wealth John's company had accumulated in a short period of time, I was far richer than I'd ever imagined possible when I'd left for the Klondike. I never found gold, but I'd found a life I hadn't even dreamed of before.

What more could any man want?

The End.

About the Author

L.A. Witt and her husband have been exiled from Spain and sent to live in Maine because rhymes are fun. She now divides her time between writing, assuring people she is aware that Maine is cold, wondering where to put her next tattoo, and trying to reason with a surly Maine coon. Rumor has it her arch nemesis, Lauren Gallagher, is also somewhere in the wilds of New England, which is why L.A. is also spending a portion of her time training a team of spec ops lobsters. Authors Ann Gallagher and Lori A. Witt have been asked to assist in lobster training, but they "have books to write" and "need to focus on our careers" and "don't you think this rivalry has gotten a little out of hand?" They're probably just helping Lauren raise her army of squirrels trained to ride moose into battle.

Website: www.gallagherwitt.com
Email: gallagherwitt@gmail.com
Twitter: @GallagherWitt

Printed in Great Britain
by Amazon